PARIS BLUES

PARIS BLUES

by

Harold Flender

FOR ENID

Cover photo by Herman Leonard

《 1 》

Body and Soul. And they were silent, attentive, enraptured. He wasn't sure why. Surely many of them had heard other versions, better versions, Coleman Hawkins, Ben Webster, Don Byas.

But they listened to the way he played it, getting out of his saxophone those special soft emotional tones, that individual phrasing that marked an Eddie Cook solo. He stood there, as always, straight and dignified, standing tall, a handsome uneven-featured dark-skinned Negro, playing with feeling but with none of the closed-eyes body-swaying tricks used by some of the other saxophonists.

The other instruments were silent. Only the piano backed him up. *Body and Soul.* It was an old number. And yet its mood and its message were still contemporary, as meaningful and universal as loneliness and unrequited love will always be, then or now, in Kansas City or New York or Paris.

They sat there quietly, as though the melody struck a responsive chord. They should have been used to this sort of thing—every Monday night they jammed into Marie's Cave on the Left Bank for the jam session—yet they sat there now without drinking or chattering or flirting, listening in silence to the soft, plaintive cry oozing out of Eddie Cook's alto sax.

They were all there, the usuals: the French oldtimers who loved jazz; the young French kids, the Saint-Germain Des-Prés boys and girls, who ate it up; the cold intellectuals—perhaps some were still Existentialists—from the Café Deux Magots; the American expatriates—the old ones tired and wan and disillusioned, the young ones energetic and bitter; the American students who loved their country and loved Paris and would go back home but always remember their year in Paris in a glorified, romanticized way.

And the sit-in musicians for tonight's jam session, hanging around after they played, some still waiting for their chance: the regulars, Negro and white, American and French, from the small clubs throughout Paris; and some from the band of the famous trumpeter Wild Man Moore, now on a tour of Europe. It was rumoured that Wild Man Moore himself might show up tonight.

It was four years since Eddie had seen him. Four years ago Wild Man Moore had taken his band on a triumphant tour of Europe's capitals, creating a sensation wherever he went and riots in Sweden by the mobs of disappointed fans who couldn't get in to hear him.

One night Wild Man Moore had unexpectedly dropped into Marie's Cave and heard Eddie play.

"Man, where you been all this time?" he had said. "You blow good. Real good! Man, why don't you come on back home? You'd blow up a storm back home, make a bundle! Where you been all my life?"

Where had he been? All his life Eddie had been worshiping Wild Man Moore, listening to every record of his he could lay his hands on, seeing the movies he was in over and over again and, one day when Wild Man Moore came to Kansas City, seeing his show all six performances, getting a headache from the lousy movie that was played in between the shows, missing supper and coming home so late his mother gave him a beating. All his life how he hoped he could one day meet the great Wild Man Moore himself, and then one day in Paris he met him, and it was too late. Too late because he knew by then that Wild Man Moore was the wrong kind of Negro, a white man's Negro, a handkerchief-head Negro.

Wild Man Moore could have done so much for his people. But whatever energies were left over after blowing his horn he poured into his heavily publicized and completely meaningless madcap antics. Like the story that had appeared in *Time* a couple of months back about Wild Man Moore and his boys showing up at a Beaux Arts Ball in New York dressed as Zulus.

Eddie had no respect for Wild Man Moore's kind of Negro. Eddie didn't want to be tolerated because he would Uncle-Tom it. He wanted to be accepted and respected—as he had been here in Paris for the past twelve years.

While he couldn't respect Wild Man Moore, he had nothing but admiration for the way he played. As a trumpeter no one could touch Wild Man Moore. And, he had to admit, there was something appealing about his outgoing warmth and generosity, the colorfully direct way he expressed himself.

It would be good if he actually showed tonight. It would be good to see him again. How the French cats would flip when he walked in.

. . . *all for you . . . body and soul*. . . . On the high key he loved to end it. As they started to applaud he blasted them with the opening note they knew meant *Sophisticated Lady*. There was another one of those standards that held them spellbound, kept them completely silent, could have led them, as the Pied Piper's tune, into the mountain cave.

The way he played held them transfixed. All but a few in the back who, he saw out of the corner of his eye, were moving around and mumbling. Newcomers. Brassy American tourists. Recently they were beginning to find their way in here. There was no escaping them.

A few angry heads turned around and *shusssshed*.

Then, unexpectedly, as profane as four-letter words in a church, came from one of the drunken American tourists: "Play *Melancholy Baby!*" And a smattering of giggles from the three or four people in his party.

Eddie looked up, continued *Sophisticated Lady*, his saxophone blaring forth louder, and angry, as though to answer the man's disturbance.

"Play *Melancholy Baby!*" the man persisted. "Nigger, I said play *Melancholy Baby!*"

It had been so long since he had heard that word. He had thought about it from time to time, as one thinks of an unpleasant childhood experience—deep in the past but with a pain that lingered and insisted upon being recalled. Now suddenly here it was. He stopped playing and looked up.

The Cave was suddenly silent. The other musicians looked at Eddie and looked at the American and put down their instruments and were ready for trouble. All except Michel, the French Negro guitarist, who clutched tightly his guitar and seemed totally unconcerned, his mind, as always lately, on a strangely haunted world of his own.

"Alvin!" the woman sitting next to the American protested. A young girl sitting at the next table, a French girl, tall and skinny with straight black hair, protested more violently. She slapped the American with all her might, her hand catching him full upon the ear.

The American stood up, reeled against the side of the table and screamed at her, "You frog bitch!" It could be heard against the epithets she was hurling at him. The other man in the party stood up to defend his American honor but thought better of it when he saw the extent to which he was outnumbered.

The musicians stood up, too, but felt there was no need yet to get into the fray. A sign from Eddie was all that was needed, but Eddie remained immobile. He felt that if he gave vent to his feelings of rage he would kill the American.

"Get out of here!" the French girl screamed at them. "Filthy Americans! Get out of here!"

The cry was taken up.

"Go home, barbarians!" a Frenchman shouted.

"Go home, American stupids!" another voice cried out.

"Come on, Alvin!" urged his wife, tugging him by the arm.

Eddie looked at Benny, the white pianist in the band. He saw the pained look on Benny's face.

He saw the puzzled looks on the faces of the American students. They were ashamed of the behavior of their drunken countryman, shocked by his language. But they didn't like what some of the French people were now saying about Americans in general, didn't like being told to go home, didn't like the looks on the faces of some of the Frenchmen.

Marie entered the room. She lived in her apartment above the night club and, Eddie figured, had probably heard the shouting. She was a statuesque Negro, beautiful and imposing, and whenever she made an entrance, even in the midst of a fracas, people had to stop and look at her.

"What's happening?" she asked.

The French waiter gestured rapidly and angrily as he told her.

She strode over to the table where the disturbance was and everyone immediately became quiet. She turned to the Americans and spoke calmly and coldly and in French, knowing that they wouldn't understand her words but would get the general idea of what she meant. "Je pense que vous ferez mieux de vous en aller tout de suite! Filez!"

She was right; they understood and they left hurriedly, a little frightened, a little surprised at hearing such perfect French spoken by someone so obviously an American Negro.

"Come up later," she said to Eddie as she passed by the bandstand on her way back to her apartment.

The place was quiet again. He started once more on *Sophisticated Lady* but now he had to play mechanically.

Eddie knew that the incident would eat at him now for days. He hated these boisterous Babbitts who had left their Lion, Elk and Rotarian Clubs for a few months or a few weeks, sometimes only a few days—most often at the suggestion of the Little Woman—to do Europe. He hated their stupidity, their grossness, their prejudice. As a Negro he'd had plenty of their prejudice back in Kansas City, even in New York. It was one of the things that made him stay in Europe after the war, these people and the way they looked at you. A few of them came over right after the war, not many, not enough to bother you. Mostly a lot of the old regulars came back and a lot of students. The students and oldtimers were okay. But now more and more of the other kind were coming over each year, so that during the past few years, especially during the summer, you couldn't get away from them. They were all over the place, the Left Bank as well as the Right Bank, in little out-of-the-way boîtes as well as the Folies Bergère and the Lido. The Paris By Night tours were bringing them in.

Eddie was aware that Marie herself was partly to blame. She had lived in Paris for twenty years, except for the war years. Before the war she had been sort of a mother-confessor to the American expatriates, a helping friend to the down-and-outers, and let it go at that. At least that was what Eddie had been told.

But since the war, especially during the past few years, with her flamboyant clothes, her odd hairdos, she had become a "character"—a sight for the American tourists to seek out and gape at, like the bearded Montmartre artists. She yielded to no one in her hatred of the American tourists, yet she was helping to bring them into her club. She was trying to prove something but Eddie didn't know what.

It was strange how every time Marie sounded off about the Americans Eddie almost felt like defending them. He hated them as much as she did, but it was her manner when she spoke about them, completely venomous, possessed with hatred, that repelled him. It was at those moments that he knew no American could ever be a match for Marie and perhaps that was why he felt what he did, a natural inclination to side with the underdog.

At the finish of the number Benny stepped down and Skinny Sam, the Negro pianist from Wild Man Moore's band, took his place. A couple of the other boys sat in too. There was a bit of a stir among the people in the audience. What were they going to hear now? Perhaps a guitar solo by Michel?

Everybody enjoyed Michel's playing, especially the French, for he was a Frenchman as well as a Negro, coming from a family long established in wealth and position.

Eddie looked at Michel. Michel's brow was furrowed, his eyes intense yet uncommunicative; he barely returned the greetings of the musicians coming up on the stand. Eddie hadn't expected to see

Michel this evening. Always unreliable, Michel had become even more so during the past few months. He had missed enough sessions for Eddie to have to consider him no longer a regular member of the band. This didn't seem to bother Michel. He had other things on his mind. Whenever Michel did somehow manage to show up, Eddie always let him play. The one reliable thing about Michel was the greatness of his guitar.

Skinny Sam waved hello to Eddie. Eddie walked over to the piano. "Wild Man coming over?" he asked.

"Maybe," replied Skinny Sam. "He's tearin' all over Paris tonight. It wouldn't surprise me none if he busted in here. But I don't know where they'd all fit. Last time I saw him he had a mob of about sixty-seventy people with him."

The newly arrived musicians settled in their places. Eddie walked to the center of the stand and gave the beat.

They let go on *High Society*. They let go on *Muskrat Ramble*. They let go on *Tiger Rag, Sister Kate, That's A Plenty, Jelly Roll Blues* and they blew the roof off, Eddie helping them, with *When the Saints Come Marching In*. All New Orleans, all Dixieland, all great, all what everybody wanted.

Eddie knew that it wasn't true that Paris never sleeps. It really does, especially at five-thirty in the morning. Except for a couple of places. While Paris slumbered in the pitch-blackness before dawn Marie's Cave couldn't have been more wide-awake as its patrons stamped their feet and clapped their hands and bobbed their heads in and out of rhythm to the screaming music of the Monday night jam session. The waiters had to move about with the agility of ballet dancers to avoid having their trays accidentally knocked out of their hands by the over-energetic jazz devotees.

And then, as suddenly as the music and the swaying and the screaming began (what now seemed so many hours ago), it suddenly stopped. One last burst of unrestrained, uninhibited, collectively improvised bedlam, and everybody knew they'd had it. The musicians

collapsed in their chairs for a minute or two, then dragged themselves
to their feet and started putting away their instruments.

The patrons, as exhausted as the musicians, started crawling
outside to the dawn, and the unimpressed waiters began clearing the
tables and piling the chairs on top of them.

Some of the fans crowded around the bandstand.

"Let's cut out for some chow," said Hank Dixon, a trombonist with
Wild Man Moore.

"Yeah, let's go, Eddie," said Skinny Sam. "Maybe we'll bump into
Wild Man Moore."

A bearded Frenchman came up to Eddie and put his arm around
him. "Eddie you were magnificent! Now you must join my friends and
me for breakfast! You must! Last week you promised you would!"

"What's he sayin'?" asked Skinny, who didn't know any French.

"He wants me to join him for breakfast," said Eddie.

"Tell the cat he can come with us," said Skinny.

"Eddie, are you going to be busy later?" asked a very pretty young
French girl. Skinny didn't have to know any French to know what she
meant.

They vied to have Eddie join them for breakfast. Eddie excused
himself on the ground that he had to drop up to see Marie. They said
they'd wait for him. He told them that it would probably take some
time, that they should go on without him, that he'd try to catch up
with them later.

"Don't look for us in the Pam-Pam Bar," said the bearded
Frenchman. "We're not going there today."

They all laughed.

"Maybe," said another Frenchman, "that's why he doesn't want to
go with us. He wants to go to the Pam Pam Bar himself for some bacon
and eggs."

Again they all laughed and he laughed with them. They knew that Eddie, like themselves, wouldn't be caught dead in the Pam-Pam Bar, a restaurant on the Champs Élysées which catered to Americans.

They hung around making jokes until Eddie finished putting away his saxophone, and then they left when they saw that he was really going up to see Marie.

"Where's Michel?" Eddie inquired. Michel was gone. He had slipped out unnoticed. No one knew where.

"The street cleaners are out working now," said Benny. "Maybe he's going after them for some of his letters of recommendation."

The musicians who knew about Michel's letters of recommendation laughed. Michel had recently acquired the notion of trying to get a job as professor of jazz at one of the Paris conservatories and, before making formal application, had started a strenuous campaign of collecting letters of recommendation. With his excellent reputation as a musician he'd had no difficulty in getting letters from some of the leading figures in European music. But he'd felt these weren't enough. He'd felt that he had to get letters from every prominent person he had ever known or met. He'd written to Toscanini, Maurice Chevalier, Benny Goodman, Dizzie Gillespie, Ted Heath, Paul Hindemith, Aaron Copland, Dimitri Mitropoulos and Dimitri Shostakovitch. He had either met them once or felt sure they had heard him play. He hadn't been able to understand why some of them hadn't sent him the letters he had asked for—other prominent figures in the music world had. Aside from musical personages he had written to other people he felt it would be helpful to have letters from—to Picasso and Cocteau, to Le Courbousier and Jean Paul Sartre and Albert Camus.

His unending quest for letters had become a laughing matter. The very idea of his teaching was absurd, anyway. He was the most irresponsible person in the world and even if he did manage to land a teaching job everyone knew that he could never hold on to it; he would never show up for his classes.

"That cat's got more letters now than the post office," said Benny.

"What's he going to do with all of them?" asked one of the musicians.

"Something about getting a job as a professor," said another one.

"If there's ever a shortage of toilet paper he can use the letters to wipe his ass," said Benny.

Eddie snapped shut his saxophone case. "Lay off him!" he said sharply to Benny. "What do you want from the poor guy?"

"I don't want nothing from him."

"Then stop trying to put him down."

"Who's trying to put him down?"

The other musicians were ready to leave. "Benny, you gonna join us for a taste?" asked one of them.

"No drinking for me this morning," said Benny. "I'm going straight home to bed."

"If you change your mind you'll know where to find us," said the musician. "S'long, Eddie."

"S'long," said Eddie.

The other musicians left and, except for a few waiters and the cleaning women, Eddie and Benny were alone. Instead of soft lights and candles the Cave was now illuminated by harsh, glaring lights. It looked garish and cheap.

"You going up to see Marie?" asked Benny.

"Yes," Eddie said.

"Boy, that Michel certainly has it made with you," Benny said. "If he doesn't feel like showing he doesn't have to. And whenever he does show you put him right to work."

"I've taken him off salary; I only pay him for the sessions he plays."

"As if he needs the dough. His family's loaded."

"I don't know what you've got against him," said Eddie.

"He gives me the creeps. He's a nice-enough guy, I suppose, mais il est fou, complètement fou. A real weirdo."

"Do you know anyone who can play a better guitar? That's all I care about."

"You mean when he shows up to play."

Eddie smiled. "You know, Benny, Michel has only the nicest things to say about you."

"That's another sign he's nuts," said Benny. "Who in his right mind would ever say nice things about me?"

"Benny, go home; you're tired. I'll see you tomorrow."

"Do you want me to put your sax away?"

"If you want to."

Benny picked up Eddie's saxophone case. "Will gladly do. And do you want me to wait for you?"

"No," said Eddie, "go home to sleep."

Eddie crossed to the door that led to the staircase to Marie's apartment. Opening the door, he glanced back over his shoulder and saw Benny gabbing with a cleaning woman. Poor Benny, thought Eddie, how he hated to go home. He let the door swing shut behind him and walked up the stairs.

The door to the apartment was closed and so Eddie knew that Varay was inside. Perhaps Marie and Varay were "busy." He hesitated a moment and then rang the doorbell. He forgot that Marie had recently installed new chimes and their sound surprised him.

If she didn't answer immediately he'd go away. Perhaps he was disturbing them. But it was her own fault if he was. She had told him to come up after he was through playing. Still, he should have known that her absence from the club meant that she was entertaining someone—Varay.

When Marie answered the door Eddie saw that she was in another dress. Yes, they had been making love. Well, what did it matter to him!

Varay sat on the sofa, dressed, as always, impeccably. His thin fingers held a cigarette. He was in his late fifties, a thin, narrow-boned man, who gave the impression of being much shorter than he actually was. He was supposed to be a real count, although he never used the title. At any rate he was quite wealthy. Eddie often wondered why he never bothered to have his teeth fixed; his front teeth were badly stained and rotted away.

Marie had known Varay for several years, but it was only during the past year that they had been seen in each other's company frequently. He was pleasant but always very cold and, certainly as far as romance went, Eddie could not understand what Marie saw in him. He was particularly repulsive when he smiled and bared his bad teeth.

"Hello, Eddie," he said, smiling.

"How are you, Varay?"

"Eddie, my love," said Marie, holding out her cheek to be kissed. Her cheek felt warm, and she smelled good, although the kiss meant nothing any more, only what it was, a perfunctory kiss on the cheek. "You look so wan, my pet," she said.

"He played all night; he should be tired," said Varay. "And I might add he played magnificently."

"I didn't see you in the club tonight," said Eddie.

"I stood behind the door listening awhile on my way up to the apartment," Varay said. "And even up here in the apartment," he continued, "your music sends out waves which penetrate ceilings and walls, which permeate the air, the atmosphere. One doesn't have to listen to it. One can feel its lively presence."

If he had said that in English, thought Eddie, it would be pure bull. In French it was still bull but somehow it sounded less objectionable.

"Would you like a drink?" asked Varay.

"No, thank you," Eddie said. Varay was certainly making himself at home, he thought.

"Eddie," said Marie, "Varay and I have had a most interesting discussion tonight."

I'll bet you did, Eddie thought. While I was blowing my guts out downstairs you were up here having a most interesting discussion. That's why you're wearing another dress now.

"The house next door is for sale," Marie continued. "Varay suggested that I buy it, expand the club. It has quite a large cellar. We could double our space."

"But property is so high in Paris now," said Eddie. "What would it cost?"

Varay smiled and said, "There's no need to have any concern about the money."

Varay flicked the ashes off his cigarette as he talked. Again Eddie wondered what Marie saw in him, and then he thought: Maybe that's it, the house next door, a newer, bigger place. Varay would foot the bill.

"What's wrong with the way the club is now?" he asked.

Marie was about to say something but Varay beat her to it. "In this business," he said, "you can't stand still. You have to expand, move forward."

"Why?"

"Oh, Eddie, my dear Eddie," said Varay, condescendingly, as if he were talking to a little boy.

"I don't see why you can't stand still if you like where you're standing," Eddie said.

"It's late," said Marie. "Perhaps this isn't a good time to talk about it. We'll talk about it tomorrow night."

"I just don't know if it's such a good idea to expand the club, that's all. I don't know what you want, what you expect to get out of it."

"Jazz is becoming more and more popular here," she said. "There are lots of new places springing up. We have to keep up with them—modernize, enlarge."

"Business has never been better," Eddie said.

"That's why now is the time to do it. It's smart business to do it now."

Eddie had never thought of the club as Marie's business. It was more her way of life. And her way of life wasn't like this, not until recently, anyhow. But now new fancy door chimes, new fancy clothes, a new fancy hairdo and a new fancy boyfriend.

"It's your club," he said. "But if you want to know how I feel about it, I've told you."

"Think about it for a while," said Marie. "You haven't given yourself time to think about it."

"All right, I'll think about it."

"By the way," said Varay, "have you been over to the *Fleur des Jardins?*"

"No," replied Eddie.

"You must go," Varay said. "There's a new band there that's simply marvelous. *Bernie Shaw.* Progressive music. It's very exciting. You don't play that kind of music, do you, Eddie?"

"No." Eddie looked at Marie, who knew he didn't play that kind of music.

"Why don't you?" Varay asked. "It's getting more and more popular."

"I don't play what's popular," Eddie said. "I play what I want to play." Again he looked at Marie. Why doesn't she shut him up, he thought. She knew how he felt about music.

"Don't you like progressive music?" asked Varay. "What are your objections to it? I find it new and rather interesting. It's quite complex, you know. Perhaps if you gave yourself a chance and listened more. . . ."

"I've no objections to it; it's just not the kind of music I care to play."

"Can you play it?" Varay asked.

"No," replied Eddie sharply. "Maybe that's why I don't play it. I can't."

"Eddie, my friend," said Varay apologetically. "I didn't mean to intimate . . ."

Eddie ignored the fact that Varay was talking. He turned to Marie. "Is that all you wanted to see me about?"

"Isn't that enough?" she replied. "It isn't every day in the week that we decide to double the space of the club."

"I'll see you tomorrow night," he said, and left the apartment.

"Your employee," said Varay, carefully emphasizing the word "employee," "is temperamental."

Marie, resting her hands on Varay's shoulders, kissed him on the tip of his nose. "You know that Eddie's been much more to me than an employee."

"And still is?"

She kissed him again, this time lightly on the lips. "Now he's only . . . a friend."

"And I?"

"Much more than a friend. But you shouldn't tell him what music to play. He's an artist and artists don't like to be told how to express themselves."

"Artist!" Varay said sarcastically.

"He is whether you like it or not. A true artist and an extremely talented one."

"Then why did you let me go on saying what I did?"

"Because," said Marie, putting her arms around Varay's neck, "it amused me."

« 2 »

ORDINARILY IT took Eddie only about an hour to unwind after work. Tonight he knew it would take much longer. The fact that Wild Man Moore hadn't showed up, the incident with the drunken American, the discussion with Benny about Michel, the way Marie was carrying on with Varay—had stirred him up inside, made him feel depressed and disappointed and angry.

The early morning air was clean and cool. He turned right on the Boulevard Raspail and walked past the Hotel Lutetia—a large hotel that had once known more elegant days. It still appeared somewhat proud, but also old and terribly tired. The street was quiet. He walked under the full blooming trees, past a few new houses, past the old chimney-topped houses—old and new alike built in the unmistakably French style, built with more than brick and mortar, built with an eye for beauty, with loving care, with impeccable taste. It was a lovely street, the Boulevard Raspail. All the streets in Paris were lovely. In his twelve years in Paris he had turned many corners, walked down many streets, and he couldn't re member one that wasn't beautiful.

He loved walking the streets of Paris. It almost always gave him a tranquil feeling.

He didn't know why Benny was down on Michel. Michel was an eccentric all right but there was no harm in him. Maybe Benny was down on him because Michel was wealthy—or at least came from a family with a lot of dough—and Benny didn't cotton to the idea of wealthy, aristocratic Negroes. No, he didn't think Benny had any prejudice, not consciously, anyway. But still, no matter how enlightened a white man was, as long as he'd been born and raised in the States some of the prejudice had to rub off. You never really knew with any of them. How could you be sure of what would happen when the chips were down?

He liked Michel, although he had to admit that his unreliability was damned annoying.

He stopped for a moment at the corner *urinoir*, holding his breath there because the odor was so strong, and then continued down the Boulevard Raspail.

And Marie, he thought. What did she want—Marie? Why the sudden grandiose plans? She used to speak with such scorn and mockery about the wealthy French decadents. Surely she realized that Varay was one of them. Varay, the stupid fool, telling him what music to play!

Marie could sleep with anyone she wanted to. He knew that at times her taste in lovers ran pretty weird. But they were always temporary relationships. If she took Varay's money to expand the club she'd be letting herself in for more than a capricious affair.

What did he care? It wasn't his club. She could let Varay take over if she wanted to. He could always get another job. He was one of the most popular musicians in Paris—all over Europe, for that matter. Agents were constantly pleading with him to do another tour of Germany. There was that club in Zurich that was always making overtures to him. And he knew he'd make out fine in any of the Scandinavian countries. The concerts he gave there three years ago had brought in a lot of dough.

No, his band was too good for him ever to have to worry if he left Marie. He could think of a dozen joints in Paris that would grab him. Why, he could open his own place. There'd be plenty of people willing to back him. He had enough money of his own to get it started. He and Benny had talked about it many times. If only Benny had been more willing they might have done it. But Benny, all he wanted to do was play piano; he didn't want any business responsibilities.

Maybe it would be a good idea to go to Zurich for a while. He had always liked the city. He hadn't been out of Paris in too long a time. And the tourist season, the hot summer, was a lousy time to be in Paris.

He crossed the Boulevard Saint-Germain to the rue du Bac and on to the Pont Royal. He paused at the center of the bridge to watch the slowly flowing waters of the Seine. One of the sightseeing boats of the Bateaux Mouches passed by, its decks empty. In a little while, thought Eddie, its decks would be crowded with stupid American tourists.

He crossed the bridge and walked into the Tuileries. The dew on the grass and flowers sparkled in the morning sun. An old park attendant, in beret and blue smock, hunted for litter. As always, the Tuileries was lovely. He could see the Arc de Triomphe on the top of the hill. Aside from the attendant, the paths in the Tuileries were deserted. Beyond, on the Champs-Élysées, he could see people moving about. He walked toward the Champs Élysées.

Zurich. He remembered the first time he was there. It was seven years ago. He had spent the afternoon walking all over the city—down by the lake, along the broad avenues, the Bahnhof-Strasse, full of so many smart shops, down the smaller streets, the Kirch-Gasse, full of so many bookstores and candy shops. It seemed by far the liveliest of the Swiss cities he had seen—bright and cheerful and friendly. About five o'clock he had wandered into a small café for a cup of coffee and some pastry. He noticed that there were several girls—all very young and all very pretty—sitting alone at separate tables. It was not until he started talking to the girl sitting next to him that he realized that they were all prostitutes. She knew a little English but when he answered in French she started speaking in French. Her French was better than her English but she spoke it with a German accent. She was a little thing, sharp-featured, dark and thin, not the kind of girl he usually liked. Still, she had a pretty face, wistful and sensitive. And when she saw that he wasn't interested in what she had to sell she continued to chat amiably with him. This never happened with French prostitutes. With them it was strictly business and they wouldn't hesitate to curse you in loud public tones for trying to waste their time.

"Aren't you interested in girls?" she asked.

"Not right now, thank you."

"Later tonight?"

Eddie smiled.

"I know you," she said. "You're the kind who's always interested. But you don't need me. You can get all you want without paying for it. You're a very handsome man."

"You're very pretty," he said. He meant it and he felt sorry for her, because he knew that even though she was quite young people wouldn't be able to say that to her much longer.

"I'm for students and old married men," she said. "And for tourists . . . for American tourists," she added, laughing. "They're my best customers. Students don't have much money. Are you a tourist?"

"No," he replied. "I'm a musician."

"I love music."

"I'm a jazz musician."

"Are you playing here in Zurich?"

"At the Tonhalle tonight."

"Oh, I wish I could hear you! But we're not allowed in those places. I like jazz, although it seems to be driving a lot of our young kids crazy. I've a younger sister. You should see the way she carries on about jazz. You don't look like a jazz musician. You look more like a young high-school professor. You'll meet a lot of nice young girls at your concert tonight. You won't have any trouble finding one to sleep with."

"I hope you're right," he said.

But she had been wrong. The concert ended at ten o'clock and there were some girls who came up to speak to him afterward, but only to speak to him. He and some of the boys from his band toured some of the clubs later, but there, too, there was nothing. He went back to his hotel room early, read a while and went to bed.

He was awakened early the next morning by a telephone call from his agent in Paris, telling him that instead of going back to Paris he should go on to Montreux, in southern Switzerland, where a three-day engagement had been arranged. He decided to get dressed and walk over to the railroad station to change the train tickets.

Outside a cold light rain was coming down. As he turned up the collar of his raincoat he saw out of the corner of his eye, across the street, the little prostitute he had met the day before at the café. She noticed him at that very same moment and they both turned around to look at each other. She said something but he couldn't hear her, because the early morning traffic on the street between them was quite noisy. Again she spoke, this time much louder, but in German, and he couldn't understand her.

"What did you say?" he yelled at her, in French.

"I asked . . . did you sleep with anyone last night?"

"No," he yelled back at her. "Did you?"

She shook her head no and for a full minute the two of them had stood there laughing in the rain.

It was a trivial incident but he knew he'd never forget it.

Paris was waking up quickly. As he walked up the Champs-Élysées the streets filled with people preparing for work. Yet they did not look busy or hurried the way they did in the States; café owners setting up their tables; newspaper vendors opening their stands; store owners re moving the iron grilles from the fronts of their shops; people on their way to work. It was funny. They had just got up and he was on his way to sleep. He touched his face and saw that he needed a shave. He was wearing the dark suit and black bow tie he played in. What was he doing on this street now, he wondered, so out of place, out of time, a creature of the night in the early morning sun?

At least there were no tourists here yet. It was too early for them. The Paris By Night tours generally didn't end until early in the morning. The tourists were still sleeping. God, how he hated them!

Walking along, he realized that he hadn't been on the Champs-Élysées in months. He lived and worked on the Left Bank and there was rarely any occasion for him to come over here. Besides, the Champs-Élysées was generally so full of American tourists that you could hear nothing but English spoken. It had changed in recent years, become more tawdry, a neon-lit, commercial street. The TWA

Airlines advertised its presence in bold, ugly letters, and further up the street the Simca and Citroën automobile companies vied to attract attention.

He found himself outside the Pam-Pam Bar and suddenly had a strong yearning for scrambled eggs and bacon and American coffee. He smiled to himself as he thought of what his friends would say if they saw him eating in the Pam-Pam Bar. But how would they ever know? Few of them ever came over here. And if he went inside, instead of eating at a table on the street, no one could possibly see him. Quickly he walked inside and sat down at an inconspicuous table in the rear of the room. He felt inwardly excited, as if he were doing something terribly naughty, like the times back in Kansas City when he used to cut school to sneak into Nigger Heaven—the second balcony at the burlesque show. Luckily there was no one inside the Pam-Pam bar.

He gave the waiter his order: a double order of orange juice, scrambled eggs and American bacon, toast and jelly, and American coffee.

His privacy was short-lived. A Negro girl walked in and sat down a few tables away from him. She was tan complexioned, rather a large girl but well proportioned, and she wore a conservative tan gabardine suit.

She gave the waiter her order in English, in a quiet, subdued, self-conscious voice. She opened her large pocketbook and Eddie saw her take out a large batch of picture postcards and a big address book. He couldn't help smiling as she started filling out the first picture postcard.

She looked up and smiled back at him.

"I'm glad to see I'm not the only tourist who's an early riser," she said cheerfully.

He frowned and replied sharply, "Je ne suis pas un touriste. J'habite à Paris."

Obviously he had spoken too rapidly for her to get what he had said.

"Would you mind repeating that more slowly?" she asked.

He threw his hands up in a typical French gesture of despair.

"I—I'm sorry," she stammered. "I thought you were an American."

She looked perplexed. He suddenly felt sorry for her. "I am an American," he said.

"Oh?" This seemed even more perplexing to her. "You speak French very well."

"I've been living here for twelve years."

"Really! How fascinating!" She seemed exhilarated by this information. She gathered up her things and moved to the table next to his.

"I hope you don't mind . . ." she said.

Eddie shrugged his shoulders as though to imply that he couldn't do anything about it even if he did mind. The girl was obviously full of the naive wonder and excitement of being for the first time in Paris. Her wide-eyed enthusiasm amused him.

"Living here in Paris for twelve years," she went on, "isn't that exciting! What do you do?"

"I'm a musician."

"Isn't that marvelous!" she exclaimed. "You must think I'm terribly bold coming over here and sitting down next to you and speaking to you like this. Ordinarily I wouldn't do such a thing, but I suppose whenever we get away from home we act differently from the way we do normally."

Her voice had dropped and the pace of her speech had slowed down on the last few words, as though she was suddenly embarrassed for her boldness. She fidgeted slightly. It was apparent that she didn't know what to say next.

Eddie looked at her large batch of postcards. "You must have many friends."

"They're for my children."

Eddie raised his eyebrows. There were at least a hundred postcards.

She giggled. "That must sound terribly funny to you. You see, I'm a teacher. I refer to my pupils as my children."

"What do you teach?"

"The lower grades."

"I guess that's a lot safer than teaching in the high schools. I understand the high school kids are going crazy in America. They're all becoming juvenile delinquents."

"It's not that bad. Whatever gave you that idea?"

"I read the papers."

"Those stories are all terribly exaggerated."

Eddie looked her over carefully. She wasn't at all bad-looking. There was nothing glamorous about her but she had definite sex-appeal. And she seemed straight. There was nothing phony or smart-alecky about her, as there was with other American girls, Negroes included.

She put her postcards and address book back into her bag. She took out a travel book. "I've been reading *Fielding's Travel Guide to Europe.* He doesn't seem to like Paris very much—Fielding." She returned the book to her bag and said, "I found out about the Pam-Pam Bar from *Asinof's Guide to Dining on the Continent.* That's a very good book. I mean it has a lot of wit in it. Do you know it?"

He shook his head no. She looked around and peered outside the restaurant.

"Maybe we ought to go outside," she said. "We can see more."

She was obviously keyed up with enthusiasm. And she didn't want to miss a trick.

"Oh, I forgot," she said. "It would be nothing new for you. How long did you say you've been over here?"

"Twelve years."

"That is a long time." She grinned sheepishly. "I've been here just two days. We arrived late yesterday afternoon. This is my first trip over here."

She brought her hand to her mouth and laughed. "I suppose I don't have to tell anybody that. It must be written all over me."

She was right, thought Eddie. Her first trip to Europe. Maybe even her first trip away from home. She'd led the sheltered life, he could see that. She probably came from a well-to-do middle-class family, the type of Negro family which tried to prove its respectability by emphasizing stuffiness and propriety and insisting that its children become doctors, ministers or teachers.

"I'm over here with a bunch of other teachers," she continued. "We're on a tour of eight countries."

The Grand Tour, thought Eddie. And when she gets home she'll be a leading authority on the European scene, with enough pointless anecdotes and empty reminiscences to last her a lifetime. He'd met the type before.

The waiter entered with their orders. If the waiter was at all surprised to see Eddie and the school teacher now seated at adjacent tables he didn't show it. As he put their food down Eddie noticed that he and the school teacher had both ordered the same things. She noticed it, too.

"You *are* American!" she said. "Bacon and eggs!"

He felt as though he had been caught doing something wrong. He began to drink his orange juice.

"How long are you going to be in Paris?" he asked.

"We're going to be here for only ten days. Then we move on to the Riviera for two days, and then down to Italy."

"*We?*"

"The other members of the tour."

"Oh yes. Are they all Negroes?"

She seemed puzzled at the question. She put down the piece of toast she was holding. "They're all schoolteachers. There are two other girls who are Negroes. Why did you ask?"

"Just curious," he replied. "All women?"

"All except one. We've one man. That is, besides the bus driver. A young fellow about twenty-two or twenty three. Poor guy, he didn't know what he was getting into. He breaks away from the group as often as he can. At least he did on the boat."

"And you? Do you break away, too?"

"Oh no," she said. "All our tours are prepaid. I haven't missed one. We visit the Louvre this morning at ten o'clock, and I wouldn't miss it for the world. I sneaked out at dawn this morning only because I couldn't wait to see Paris. I've been walking around for over two hours!"

"So have I," Eddie said.

"You have?" she asked, surprised.

He was immediately sorry that he had told her. It was none of her business. Nevertheless he continued: "Except I haven't gone to bed yet. I just got through working."

"Are you a jazz musician?"

"That's right," he said. "How'd you know?"

"I guessed," she said. "I bet there are an awful lot of jazz musicians living in Paris."

"Not only musicians," he said, abruptly. "There are quite a few Negro artists here, too. And writers, and students, and professors and doctors."

He wondered why he continued talking to her. She seemed naive and superficial.

"Well, you needn't act so angry about it," she said.

"I'm not angry. It's just that so many people think in stereotypes. An American Negro living in Paris, and he has to be a jazz musician. That's typical."

"I'm hardly the one to think in stereotypes," she protested. "I'm well aware of the progress our people have made."

"I'm glad to hear that," he said.

They continued to eat. Her gay enthusiasm suddenly seemed somewhat dampened. She no longer smiled. She wiped her lips with a napkin, took a sip of coffee, and with a marked look of curiosity asked, "Where do you *originally* come from?"

She put an elbow on the table and supported her chin with her hand. She looked intense as she leaned toward him, as though she didn't want to miss a word of what he had to say. Her rapt attention made him feel slightly un comfortable.

"I was born in Kansas City," he replied, "but I lived in New York for a few years before going into the army and coming over to Europe."

"I originally came from Pleasantville, Louisiana," she said.

"I never heard of it."

"I didn't think you would. I doubt that it's even on a map."

"And I bet it wasn't very pleasant."

"As a matter of fact, it wasn't."

"Neither was Kansas City—as a matter of fact."

"But I like Chicago. That's where I'm living now. I like Chicago very much. The school I teach in is a bit run down, but on the whole the kids are nice. And I have my own apartment. And, well, there's a lot going on in Chicago all the time."

"It's lively all right. It swings. But ugly. You can't compare it to any of these European cities."

"No," she admitted, "it isn't a very pretty city. It certainly can't compare to Paris . . . the little I've seen of it, anyway."

"Have you ever been to San Francisco?" he asked.

"No."

"San Francisco and New York are the only cities in America that have any of the sophistication that you find in European cities. Are you a White Sox fan?"

"A what?"

"A White Sox fan. Chicago White Sox."

"Oh!" she caught on. "No . . . I'm afraid I'm not much of a baseball fan."

"I used to be quite a Giant fan," he said. "That's the one thing I miss about the States, the baseball games."

"Is that the only thing?" she asked, looking down at the food.

"And the bacon and eggs," he added, smiling. "And the coffee. But I used to go to the baseball games whenever I could. I miss New York, too, once in a while."

He looked up as he spoke, not at her, but past her, at nothing in particular.

"It's a funny thing," he said. "I hated New York. I spent five years beating my head against a stone wall in New York, trying to get some place with my music. During the day I used to work pushing a hand truck down in the fur market. At nights I used to study at Juilliard. I lived with my aunt who worked as a domestic. Every day she'd go up to Burnside Avenue in the Bronx and stand on the corner of the slave market waiting to be looked over and maybe picked up. When the war came along she got a steady job and made me quit work and go to school full-time. I was great at school but I couldn't get a job . . . not playing the kind of music I wanted to. I never made it in New York, and I hated it. And yet now I think I'd kind of like to see Lenox Avenue again, and 125th Street, and Central Park, and the Village. I wouldn't even mind seeing that rat-infested trap we called home—providing I wouldn't have to live there again."

"I knew some kids who went to Juilliard, " she said. She mentioned their names but they were after his time and he didn't know any of them.

"Do you know New York?" he asked.

"I've been there a few times. Short visits. I really don't know it. We were there for four days before the boat left."

"Did you ride on the top of a Fifth Avenue bus?"

"They don't have those any more. They don't have any double-deckers."

"They don't?" He was disappointed.

"I don't think they've had those since the end of the war."

"Don't tell me they've done away with the Staten Island Ferry, too!"

"No," she laughed. "That's still there. As a matter of fact I took a ride on it. It was just about ten days ago."

"Still a nickel?"

"Still a nickel."

He offered her a cigarette.

"I've never seen that kind before," she said. "What kind is it?"

"Players. They're English."

"I don't smoke much," she said, "but I'll try one of these."

He lit it for her. She took a puff, and said, "You sound like you're homesick to me."

"Are you kidding?" he said. "I may think about New York once in a while, but Paris is the greatest city in the world. I wouldn't think of living any place but here. Why, do you know, I think I must've walked over every foot of this city, and there's not an inch of it I don't love. Except maybe this street, because it's gotten so commercial."

"And filled with so many American tourists?" she asked.

"Sometimes that, too."

"Do you walk a lot?"

"Yes, I do," he replied. "I usually spend at least a couple of hours a day just walking. As I said, I've walked all over this city, from Porte d'Orleans to Clichy, and all of it's beautiful. It's the only place I've ever felt at home, accepted, a human being."

"Do you walk alone?" she asked.

"Yes," he answered. "Sometimes with Benny Levine. He's the only other guy in the band who likes to walk. He's the pianist. We've got a mixed group."

He paused. "Mostly I walk alone."

"That's very interesting," she said. "A friend of mine who's a psychologist, actually a psychiatric case worker, said that people who like to walk alone a lot are really searching for their mothers."

"My mother's been dead for twenty years." She reminded him of the kids he knew at Juilliard. So concerned with psychology. So unlike the French.

"Of course," she continued, "my friend went to the New York School for Social Work, and they're very Freudian."

"Everything, of course, has to have a Freudian explanation."

"I don't necessarily agree with everything she says. I thought it would be interesting to give you her explanation, though."

Eddie ordered a second cup of coffee, and although she hadn't finished her first she ordered a second cup, too.

"Haven't you been back to the States at all?" she asked.

"Not since the war," Eddie replied. "I came over here in 1943 with the army, was discharged in '46, right here in Paris, and I've been here ever since."

"Do you do well here? I mean, I don't mean to get personal . . ."

"Right now I'm playing at a boîte on the Left Bank called Marie's Cave. Come over some night."

"Maybe I will." She looked at her watch. "I'll have to get going pretty soon. My roommate will have a fit when she wakes up and finds I'm not there. She's the worrying type. A real character."

"Is she a Negro?" asked Eddie.

"No, she's white. Why do you ask?"

"I was just wondering."

"She's really something. She's about sixty. She's extremely funny, although I must admit most of the time she doesn't mean to be."

"What other countries are you going to?"

"Italy, Germany, Austria, Switzerland, Lichtenstein, Spain and England."

"All in—how long?"

"Ten weeks."

"I've been to all of them," he said.

"Even Lichtenstein?"

"Even Lichtenstein."

"Is it nice?"

"It'll do. For a day."

"That's all we're staying there for."

"How long are you going to stay in Spain?"

"About a week. England's our last stop. Then home."

"Then home," he repeated.

"Home and school." She looked at her bag, then up at him again.

"You know," she said, "I still think you're homesick."

Suddenly the expression on his face changed. He frowned, almost sneered at her. "For what? For what's happening in the South?"

"I think it's wonderful," she said.

"Wonderful?" He was incredulous.

"I mean at last people are speaking up, taking some action, demanding what's right."

"A lot of good it'll do!"

"It will do good," she said firmly. "A lot of good!"

Now she was no longer the naive, exuberant tourist. Now she was the arbitrary schoolteacher.

"How many lynchings have there been there recently?" he snarled. "How many more murderers have been let off after beating little Negro kids to death? How many more homes have been blown up? It's a great country!"

He signaled to the waiter, who came over and gave him both checks. He put down enough money to pay for his.

"I'll see you some time," he said to her, and left.

She was startled by his reaction, by the abrupt way he left. How very rude, she thought. Even the waiter seemed embarrassed. She fumbled in her purse to find some money to pay the bill.

I didn't get his name, she thought. And he didn't ask me mine.

« 3 »

WHEN CONNIE returned to her hotel, Lillian, her roommate, was in the lobby nervously pacing back and forth. She was a tall, gaunt woman, sixty years old. She wore her hair in a short neat bob, and her only concession to cosmetics was a faint suggestion of lipstick.

"Where were you!" she cried out in a high-pitched voice.

The concierge behind the desk smiled in amusement. Connie felt embarrassed.

"Out walking," said Connie, as nonchalantly as possible. She felt resentful that she had to answer to Lillian.

"Why didn't you tell me?" Lillian complained. "I didn't know what had happened to you!"

"You were fast asleep," Connie explained. "I didn't want to disturb you." She looked around. Luckily, aside from the concierge, there was no one in the lobby.

"You should have left a note on the table," said Lillian. "Or told the man at the desk or one of the girls. I was frantic. I called everyone to find out where you were!"

"Oh, Lillian . . ."

"I couldn't imagine what happened to you! You must never wander off alone like that again: After all, this is Paris!"

"Where is everybody?" asked Connie.

"They're in the dining room having breakfast. I couldn't eat, I was so nervous worrying about you. Come on, let's go inside."

"I've already had breakfast."

"But I asked the waiter. He said he didn't see you."

Just my luck to end up with a neurotic fusspot for a roommate, thought Connie. "I stopped off at a restaurant on the Champs-Élysées."

"But, my dear, all our meals are prepaid. You're supposed to eat with us at the hotel."

"Oh, Lillian, you don't have to stick to every letter of the rules."

"Well, you might as well come in and have another breakfast now. You've paid for it."

"But I told you I've already had breakfast." She was impatient with Lillian. "I'm going up to the room for a minute. You go on inside."

"Are you sure you'll be all right?"

"Of course," said Connie.

Lillian started for the dining room, then turned around. "Connie, wait . . ."

Connie was at the foot of the stairs. Lillian crossed to her and, glancing around to make sure no one was within earshot, asked, "Are you going to the bathroom?"

Connie wasn't. She just wanted to get away from Lillian and be by herself a while. To avoid further conversation she nodded that she was and started up the stairs.

"Wait a minute!" said Lillian.

Connie halted. Lillian walked up the steps to her. "Open my brown valise and take out my roll of toilet paper. The French toilet paper is dreadfully rough. And don't forget to wipe the seat with disinfectant. I did it last night but it can't hurt to do it again. You never know who may have used it since." In a tone of self-pity she added, "I wish I weren't so constipated. You don't know how lucky you are." She hurried off to the dining room.

In her room Connie switched her wallet and passport from the large bag she had been carrying to a smaller purse. She also took out the inexpensive 35mm camera she had bought just before the trip. She knew that carrying the camera around would make her feel very much the tourist, but she knew also that if she didn't, later on, after the trip was over, back in the States, she'd regret not having taken pictures.

The room she and Lillian shared was large but quite old and musty. The rug on the floor was worn shabby, the light fixtures were probably the very same ones installed when electricity first replaced gas, and two dirty, ancient gold-colored quilts lay on top of the scarred gold-colored beds. The wallpaper was peeling near the ceiling and there were water stains in one corner.

Well, what could you expect for ten weeks in Europe, including the fare, for $1,000? And the company that arranged the tour had to make a profit on that, too! What surprised her was that the windows were kept sparkling clean and the bathroom down the hall was very clean, too.

She smiled to herself, as she recollected Lillian, at dinner the night before, telling the girls about the bidet. "I've read about them," Lillian had said, "and I've been told about them, but this is the first time I've ever seen one! Do you really think they're actually used?" What a character!

And what a character was that musician fellow, thought Connie. Awfully good-looking. But terribly neurotic, too. Still, there was something attractive about him.

She sat down on the edge of the bed and thought about him until it was time to go downstairs again.

As Connie entered the lobby she saw that most of the girls were already seated there, waiting for a few stragglers from the dining room. Martin Weiner, the one boy on the tour, sat alone looking as quietly unhappy as ever. Mrs. Vogel, the tour guide, was there, as was Peter, the Belgian bus driver. Mrs. Vogel was talking to a young, slightly plump, bespectacled man. When she saw Connie she turned away and said to her, "Now Connie, I do wish next time you drift off alone you'd let us know where you're going. Lillian was simply distraught over not knowing what had happened to you."

"I went for a little walk," said Connie, annoyed at Mrs. Vogel's making such a fuss. "My God!"

"As you know," said Mrs. Vogel, "we have several hours set aside each day for unplanned activities and of course you can do whatever you like then, but as I've told you repeatedly during our orientation lectures on the boat we do request that you tell us where you are going." The plump, bespectacled man smiled at Connie condescendingly.

"Please girls," continued Mrs. Vogel, "everybody remember that. Always leave word where you're going."

On the boat coming over, aside from the three one hour orientation lectures, Mrs. Vogel had let them pretty much alone. But now Connie was suddenly aware of how much like some of her bureaucratic school supervisors was Mrs. Vogel. She had hoped to get completely away from that sort of thing on this trip to Europe. She now saw that Mrs. Vogel would be a constant link to the atmosphere of school.

"Is everybody here?" asked Mrs. Vogel. Everybody was there.

"Girls, I want you to meet Mr. Luften."

"Hi, girls," said Mr. Luften, beaming broadly.

"I'm always saying 'girls,'" interrupted Mrs. Vogel. "What I mean to say is 'girls and Mr. Weiner.'"

Connie looked at Martin. He winced, slid down a few inches in his chair and looked even unhappier than usual. She sympathized with him; at the same time she couldn't help but be amused at the humor of the situation.

"Mr. Luften," continued Mrs. Vogel, "is affiliated with Teachers Tours, Inc. . . ."

"And about two dozen others," interrupted Mr. Luften, chuckling with pride.

"Yes . . ." Mrs. Vogel was obviously annoyed that he had informed them of this. "He's an authority on art history and it's our good fortune to have him as our guide for this morning's tour of the Louvre."

"The time to wander off by yourself in Paris," said Mr. Luften, "isn't early in the morning, but early in the evening." He winked at Connie and the girls giggled. Connie forced a weak smile; he was a stupid fool.

"Girls," he continued, "er, I mean girls and Mr. Weiner . . ." Again a laugh. "In a little while we're going to visit the greatest art museum in the world, the Louvre. The halls of the Louvre—halls of antiques, of painting and sculpture, of art objects and furniture—show man's cultural accomplishments from earliest history to the end of the nineteenth century. I thought before we went over there I'd give you a little bit of the history of the Louvre, its background."

Oh no, thought Connie. She was reminded of a course in music appreciation she had taken in her freshman year at college, where the teacher had insisted on talking and talking and talking about music, practically never letting them listen to any of it. Why couldn't they just go over to the Louvre and see the paintings? Was this what the entire tour was going to be like?

"First of all," asked Mr. Luften, "does anyone know the meaning of the word 'Louvre'—where the word 'Louvre' comes from?"

The group looked at one another. No one seemed to know. Finally Lillian raised her hand.

"Put your hand down, young lady," said Mr. Luften, "because you don't know the answer."

Referring to a woman of sixty as "young lady" drew a few titters.

"You don't know the answer," said Mr. Luften, "because no one knows the answer. The truth is no one knows what the word actually means or where it comes from."

"That's just what I was going to say," said Lillian.

Mr. Luften looked skeptical.

"I was!" insisted Lillian and she looked at Connie. For once they both obviously agreed on something: what an obnoxious man was Mr. Luften.

He rambled on and on, giving them an outline of the history of the museum, information he had probably learned by rote from some pamphlet. He made it all sound very dull and Connie couldn't keep her mind on what he was saying. Every once in a while she caught a date, a name . . . 1214 . . . Philip Augustus . . . Charles V in 1364 . . . Francis I . . . Henry IV . . . Louis XIII . . . Louis XIV . . . Napoleon . . . the Richelieu Pavilion . . . It was mostly a dull jumble of dates and names and she kept thinking of the Pam-Pam Bar and the jazz musician she had met there.

Looking around, Connie observed that the others were trying hard to appear interested in what Mr. Luften was saying. After all, these were important historical facts relating to the background of what they were about to see. But actually they too were restless and eager to see the Louvre for themselves.

Peter, the bus driver, was the only one with a contented look on his face. Indeed, he was smiling rather happily. He didn't understand English too well.

After Mr. Luften finished his lecture they were herded into the bus and driven to the Louvre.

The lobby of the museum was full of all sorts of groups: American tourists, French schoolchildren, German and Italian and British tourists, French art students. There were many people who weren't attached to large groups but were by themselves or with one or two other people. Connie envied them. Some of her fellow-teachers got quite excited over the presence of some bearded, sandaled artists. And they were quite disappointed when they were told they'd have to check their cameras.

Connie and two of the others wandered over to one of the long counters at the side of the lobby at which were sold prints, art books, posters and postcards.

"Let's stick together, everybody!" admonished Mrs. Vogel. "You'll have fifteen minutes to buy souvenirs at the end of the tour!"

They were marched up the stairs to the entrance to the main gallery. At the head of the stairs, before a familiar statue, Mr. Luften stopped them. "Now here's something you've all seen hundreds of times," said Mr. Luften, "in photographs, that is. Now for the first time you're seeing the beautiful statue itself."

It was the famous "Victory of Samothrace," and even Mr. Lufton's banter couldn't distract Connie from enjoying it.

She was thrilled, too, a moment later, when they entered the main hall of the Louvre. Now, she felt, for the first time in her life she knew the true meaning of the word *magnificence.* How lucky the jazz musician was to be able to live in Paris. She wondered if he ever visited the Louvre or cared about art.

As they marched through gallery after gallery, seeing the great masterpieces of Raphael, of Leonardo da Vinci, of Titian, Rubens and Van Dyck, all the drawings, engravings, antiques, bronzes, ancient and modern sculptures, tapestries, and furniture collections, Connie's feet began to feel tired, her eyes strained from seeing too much art, her ears dulled from hearing too many facts, dates and names incessantly droned at them by tireless Mr. Luften. The first breathtaking effect of the Louvre was wearing off and her mind began to wander back more and more to the musician she had met early that morning. How strange he was. So disturbed and discontented and yes—so very rude; yet, she had to admit again, not without a good deal of attractiveness. She was always drawn toward the troubled, disturbed and disturbing type; it was the dismay of her relatives and friends. She wondered whether she would ever see him again.

❰❰ 4 ❱❱

EDDIE SAT in his pajamas on the edge of the bed. He knew that if he was to sleep he would have to lower the blinds to keep the bright sunlight from pouring into the room, but he felt too tired to get up and cross over to the window and he felt too tired to lie down and go to sleep. Too tired to sleep. It had happened before. It was happening more and more frequently. He had walked too much. All the way over to the Champs-Élysées and the Pam Pam Bar. All the way back to the Left Bank and to his apartment.

It was a small but ideal bachelor's apartment: a bedroom, a living room, a bathroom, a kitchen and a small balcony overlooking the broad and bustling Avenue du Général Leclerc. It was bright—a cleaning woman who came in four times a week kept it spotlessly clean—and it was furnished in modern Swedish, part of a deal Eddie made the first time he played in Stockholm. On the white painted walls were hung inexpensive prints which he had picked up from the bookstalls along the Left Bank of the Seine.

Eddie enjoyed the brightness of the place, and the first thing he usually did when he awoke in the morning was to pull up the blinds and let the sunlight in. He knew that now he should shut the sunlight out if he wanted to sleep, and he did want to sleep, but he had no inclination to draw the blinds.

The schoolteacher he met had annoyed him. Naive and superficial, that's what she was, like so many of the other schoolteachers and social-workers and secretaries who came over from the States. Why did he even waste his time speaking to them? Yet he always did. Sometimes it was they who spoke first to him, seeking out his friendship. But just as often, he had to admit, it was he who first approached them. And it always ended the same way, in disappointment, with his running away from them, escaping from them, avoiding them if he happened to see them later.

With the Europeans it was different. He could be friends with them. And with the boys in the band, some of them, and with some other Americans who had been over here a long time.

He couldn't stop thinking of the school teacher. Maybe it was because he hadn't had a girl for a few weeks. He thought of calling up Nadine. She was probably home now; she'd come over. On second thought, he really didn't feel like it. He was too tired. And he had lost all interest in Nadine, anyway. Once they were through making love there was nothing to say to her, nothing to do.

He dragged himself up from the edge of the bed and crossed over to the window. The Avenue du Général Leclerc was alive with people, cars, buses and trucks. It was alive and noisy, even though the Prefect of Police had banned the honking of auto horns. At times he missed the horn-honking. It had never bothered him, never kept him from sleeping. It was like an atonal composition. Now all the horns of Paris were quiet. But the motors still spat and coughed, and the brakes still screeched, and the people still talked loudly.

He put on his robe, stepped out on his tiny balcony and gazed down the avenue. He remembered the last time he had stood on the balcony—a few days ago, in the early morning. The street was quiet then, almost deserted. He had awakened from a bad dream in which he saw himself back in New York, wandering around Times Square, poor and out of work, his clothes seedy, the streets dirty and full of unfriendly, hard-faced people. To escape he bought a ticket to a cheap Times Square movie, and as he was entering the frightening darkness of the theatre he woke up. He felt tremendously relieved as he realized that he wasn't back in New York, but here in Paris. To forget his dream he had gone out on his balcony and breathed the air of Paris, basked in its warm sunlight, took in as much of the city as the eye could see. A dream of being back in America. A nightmare. And *she*, the teacher, had said he was homesick!

He went back into the room, took off his robe, lowered the blinds and got into bed. His bones ached with tired ness but he still continued to feel restless.

The telephone rang. "Bonjour, Eddie. Comment ça va?"

It was Michel. If it had been anyone else he might have invited him over. But he didn't feel like seeing Michel now.

"What are you doing, Eddie?" asked Michel.

"I was in bed," replied Eddie.

"I tried to get you before," said Michel.

"I didn't get in until a little while ago."

"I just called to say hello and find out how you were," said Michel. "I didn't get a chance to speak to you tonight."

"I'm fine, thanks," said Eddie. He thought it odd that Michel was reticent in person but would often talk for hours on the phone. He had no desire at the moment for a long phone conversation with Michel. "I better get back to sleep," he said. " I have to get up in a little while."

There was no immediate reply, and Eddie thought that he might have hurt Michel's feelings. He didn't want to do that. "I looked for you after we finished playing tonight," he said, "but you had left."

"Can I come over now?" Michel asked. "There's something I'd like to see you about."

"Must it be right now? I'm dog-tired. You must be tired, too. We had a long night."

Again there was silence at the other end of the phone. "Is it anything urgent?" asked Eddie.

"Picasso hasn't answered me yet, I surely thought there'd be a letter from him this morning. And so I've written him again."

The letters again.

"Do you think Picasso is ill?" asked Michel.

"I don't know," Eddie said. "I haven't heard anything to that effect."

"Then why do you suppose he doesn't answer me? I met him, you know. He should remember me. He heard me play. He complimented me afterwards."

"Yes, I know," said Eddie. "Look, don't worry about it. You don't need his letter. You have enough letters if you want to get a job. You should apply before all the jobs are filled for the Fall term."

"A letter from Picasso would be very impressive," Michel insisted.

"No more than some of the letters you've gotten from famous musicians," Eddie pointed out. "After all, Picasso is no expert in music."

"Why do you suppose he hasn't answered me?"

"Look, Michel," said Eddie. "Let's talk about it later. I've got to get some sleep now. Good-by."

He waited to hear Michel's good-by. He didn't, and hung up anyway.

Eddie wondered whether Michel really believed in what he was doing or was just trying to establish himself as a character. In some Parisian circles people would go to any lengths to have some characteristic that would set them apart from their friends, some eccentricity that would make them stand out from the rest; sometimes the more outlandish, the better. Everyone knew it was done just for the effect; no one took it seriously. But somehow Michel didn't seem the type.

Michel had everything—money, talent, born and raised in France where nobody cared about the color of your skin. And yet he had a screw loose.

You just couldn't win.

Eddie closed his eyes. He hoped that he'd be able to fall asleep.

« 5 »

BENNY, AFTER hours of tossing and turning and feeling tense and having all the horrible thoughts he always had in this insomnious state that somehow never looked quite so bad in retrospect, was at last suddenly able to let go and feel relaxed all over, and hear his brain saying okay, that's enough torture for the moment, I'll let you sleep now, Benny.

The twilight zone, drifting into sleep, good-by to miserable sleeplessness, he'd beaten it another time, nothing to disturb him now, nothing, nothing, except an unexpected rapping on the door, a light rapping, nothing urgent about it, a casual and unimportant rapping, but clear and persistent enough for him to notice it, to be bothered by it, a small rapping that kept him from crawling into sleep, each small rap setting up a huge roadblock at the end of his road to sleep, so that he couldn't reach it, no, not now, not when he had to answer the door.

Damn!

He was fully awake.

Who the hell could that be!

He got out of bed and opened the door and stared in amazement at Michel.

"What the hell are *you* doing here?"

"I want to show you the letter I've written to Picasso."

"For chrissakes, Michel, it's ten o'clock in the morning. I was just beginning to fall asleep."

"Can I come in?"

"What do you want? . . . Okay, come in."

Benny's small one-room apartment was, as usual, messy: clothes strewn all over the place, unwashed dishes on top of the table, magazines and newspapers on the chairs.

"What do you want, Michel?"

"Can I sit down?"

He cleared off a chair for Michel. Michel sat down and took a letter out of his pocket.

"I've just written this letter to Picasso."

"Jesus, man," said Benny, "is that what you got me out of bed for!"

"He never answered my first. On the other hand he may never have received the other letter—someone may have interfered with its reaching him—but I don't know if I should say this in the letter."

He handed the letter to Benny.

"My dear M. Picasso," read Benny, "I hope you will forgive me for impinging on your valuable time, but a matter of . . ."

He stopped and angrily shook the letter in his hand. "For chrissakes, Michel!"

"Don't you see how important it is that I get a letter of recommendation from him? It would insure my getting a job teaching at the Conservatory."

"Why should Picasso write to you? Does he even know you?"

"Yes, he met me. Cocteau brought him into the club one day. He said he liked the way I played very much. He said—"

"How long ago was that?"

"About three years ago," replied Michel.

"And you think he'll remember now? What's wrong with you, Michel!"

"He'll remember. He was very friendly at the time. He—"

"I want to get back to bed," said Benny. "So, if you don't mind, Michel . . ."

"I've written again to Stravinsky, too,"

"Look," interrupted Benny. "Why don't you forget all about your letters for a while? Get your mind on something else—like dames. You never seem to go out with dames like the rest of us. Look, I could fix you up with a couple of nifty broads—nothing professional, they just love to put out. Maybe that's all you need."

"There are more important things that concern me now," said Michel.

"Why the hell are you so het-up about getting a job teaching? What's wrong with playing jazz?"

"How long can one continue to play jazz in nightclubs? One must look to the future."

"For chrissakes, Michel, you're a young guy. You've just started. Look at me. I'm in my forties; I've been making this noise for over twenty years now and I'm just beginning to get the feel of it, just beginning to hear the sound."

"Oh, I'll continue playing," said Michel. "But in the Conservatory. Playing in nightclubs no longer appeals to me. I have to agree with my family about nightclubs."

Benny stood up and turned his back on Michel. "You're nuts. I swear to God you're nuts."

"Don't you want to read the letter?"

"Not particularly." He handed it back to Michel. Michel looked hurt.

"Do you want a drink?" asked Benny.

"No, thank you."

A bottle and some glasses were on the table in the center of the room. Benny poured a drink and offered it to Michel. "Go on, take it; it'll be good for you."

"I said I didn't want it," said Michel.

Benny gulped it down himself. "Do you want some fruit? There's some fruit in the ice-box."

"I don't want anything, thank you," said Michel, his arms hanging down wearily on the sides of the chair, the open letter in his hand.

"That's right, sit there and pout, try to make me feel sorry for you! Well, man, I don't feel sorry for you one bit, you hear!"

Michel didn't move. He looked up at Benny balefully.

"Why should I?" continued Benny. "Christ, you shouldn't even have the talent you have. It's such a waste with you. . . . We never know if you're going to show up on time or if you're going to show at all. You don't know what it is to have to work for a living. No, you'll never get me to feel sorry for you. Picasso and Stravinsky didn't answer you! The idea!"

Slowly Michel folded his letter and put it back in his pocket. "I guess I had better go now."

"I guess you better. Coming in here like a nut, bothering me with your letters."

Michel tapped the outside of the pocket into which he had slipped his letter. "I'm going to mail this to him just the same. He'll answer me."

"Who cares!" exploded Benny. "I couldn't care less!"

Michel sat there without moving, his face somber, his thoughts obviously far away.

What did this creep want from him? Benny wondered. He hardly ever had anything to do with him. The Americans living in Paris were supposed to be lost, but Benny had never seen anyone as lost as this French cat. He'd never understood French Negroes, anyway, the few of them he'd met.

Michel stood up and walked out of the apartment. Benny got back into bed. That crazy sonofabitch, he thought, coming up here with his goddamn letters. Eddie so friendly toward him, treating him like a big brother. Sure Michel was a great guitarist, but he was also a big nut.

Maybe Eddie was infatuated with the idea of his being French and coming from a snooty family, although Eddie was usually not impressed with that type of jazz. Actually, Eddie didn't bother too much with Michel, hardly ever saw him socially. Eddie was much closer to him than he was to Michel, there was no question about that.

《 6 》

IT WAS on their fifth day in Paris that Connie and Lillian found themselves in Marie's Cave.

Mr. Luften's tours, it turned out, included more than art galleries. To those tourists he thought would be interested he offered special Paris by Night guided tours. When he approached Mrs. Vogel's group, Connie and two other girls said that they were interested. Although they did not relish Mr. Luften as their guide they found the price for visiting four nightclubs extremely reasonable. Martin Weiner felt that he needed no guide to show him Paris, and Lillian went along rather than spend the evening alone in her hotel room.

A sign outside Marie's Cave announced that Eddie Cook and his Band were featured inside, but while the name Marie's Cave did strike a vaguely familiar note Connie thought that perhaps she might have seen it advertised on a poster or read about it in one of the guide books—the name Eddie Cook meant absolutely nothing to her for the moment.

Lillian held on to Connie's arm for moral as well as physical support as Mr. Luften led them down the steps to the entrance.

The band was playing as they entered and Connie was startled to see Eddie on the bandstand. She now knew why the name Marie's Cave had sounded familiar to her.

Seeing him was a pleasant surprise. Somehow none of her experiences in Paris had been as meaningful to her as her encounter with the jazz musician. She had thought about him a great deal, but although she knew he played in a nightclub she never expected it to be one of the four on her Paris by Night tour; indeed the very first one.

The club was dimly lit. Candles atop checkered table cloths. They were led to their table and as they sat down Connie caught Eddie's eye.

She wondered whether he would remember her. Perhaps he would and pretend he didn't.

At the end of *How High the Moon* there was mild applause. Eddie put his sax down and walked off the stand. Benny gave the beat for *Talk of the Town*.

Eddie crossed directly to Connie's table.

"Hello," he said. "I see you remembered."

"Remembered what?" she asked.

"Where I was playing."

"As a matter of fact I forgot all about it," she replied. "We just happened to come in as part of our tour."

He seemed disappointed, a little hurt. She introduced him to Mr. Luften, Lillian, and the other two teachers. All were quite surprised to see that Connie knew the band leader. She introduced him by name, as if she knew it well, not as though, as was the case, she remembered it from seeing it displayed outside the club. She felt proud of this subterfuge until he spoiled it by asking, "By the way, what's your name?"

"Connie—Connie Mitchell," she said, embarrassed.

He asked her to dance and she excused herself from the table.

It was relatively early in the evening for Marie's Cave and the place had not begun to get crowded. Only half the tables were occupied and there were only two other couples on the floor. He danced well and she let him hold her close, even though she knew that her companions were staring at them.

"How do you like Paris?" he asked.

"Not particularly." She felt his arms relax a little.

"Are you serious?"

She saw how easily upset he became. Good, she thought. He had been rude to her, had made her feel uncomfortable. Now they were even. Besides, she meant what she said. "Actually, I'm not terribly disappointed," she went on, "because a few of my friends who've been here told me what it would be like. "

"Have you seen much of Paris?"

"Enough. I can't wait to go on to Italy. I've heard that the people are much nicer there."

"How many Frenchmen have you actually spoken to? You don't even know the language."

"I know a little French. The people here don't even try to understand you. They run away from you. Unless they expect a tip."

"You're not being very fair," he said. "You've met only those Frenchmen who come into contact with Americans. Naturally they're antagonistic."

"Why, *naturally?*"

"Well," he said, "you must admit that the typical American tourist is pretty obnoxious. "

"Am I obnoxious?" she asked.

"I didn't mean you."

"How about my three friends? Do they look obnoxious?"

He swung her around so that he could look at them. "They look all right."

"Now who's being unfair?" she asked. "How many American tourists have you met?"

"I keep meeting them all the time," he said.

The music ended and for a moment Connie feared that Eddie would escort her back to the table but he signaled the pianist and the band started playing again. *The Lamp Is Low*. They continued dancing.

"I know how you feel about America," said Connie. "One thing you have to admit, though, America has the feeling of being alive, of being contemporary. Paris has the feeling of being passé. It's living on its memories."

"It's become a cliché—what you just said about France living on the past."

"That doesn't make it any less true, does it?"

He again held her close as they danced, but this time she perceived a feeling of tension, of antipathy.

For a moment they danced without talking, then he said to her, "If you knew my Paris you wouldn't talk that way."

"I'm open-minded," she said. "Where is your Paris? How do I get to see it?"

"I'll show it to you," he said. "Tonight-after I'm through working."

"What time is that?"

"We close at four."

"Four in the morning?"

"I'll leave early tonight," he said. "Hang around until about half-past twelve. Then we'll take off."

"But we're supposed to visit three other nightclubs tonight. It's all part of the tour."

"You'll never see Paris on a tour," he said. "Not that kind of tour."

"I'll speak to my friends."

"If we go, just the two of us," he said. "No friends."

"All right," she said.

When the dance ended Eddie went back to the bandstand.

"Who's he?" asked Mr. Luften.

"Just a friend," replied Connie, as casually as she could. "Incidentally," she continued, "I'm going to stay on here."

"But we've three other nightclubs to visit," protested Mr. Luften. "And two of them have lavish floorshows!"

"I'd prefer if you'd go on without me," said Connie.

"Can she get a refund on the other three clubs?" asked Lillian.

"I'm afraid not," said Mr. Luften. "It's a package deal. You better come along with us. Mrs. Vogel wouldn't like it one bit if she knew we left you here alone."

"Oh, Mrs. Vogel!" said one of the other schoolteachers. "You stay if you want to stay, Connie!"

"Well," said Mr. Luften, "of course I can't force you to come along with us if you don't want to."

"What about me?" cried Lillian. "I came because of you, Connie. I wanted to watch out for you. Now you want to stay here by yourself and goodness knows what will happen to you."

"Nothing's going to happen to me," said Connie. "You go on with the rest, Lillian, and have fun!"

"Fun!" exclaimed Lillian. "This is no fun for me!"

"See the fuss you're causing," said Mr. Luften. "You better come along with us."

"I don't want to cause any fuss," said Connie, "and I'm not going to go along with you. I'm sorry, but I want to remain here."

The band ended its set and took a break. Eddie and Benny came over to the table, pulled up chairs and sat down. Benny sat next to Lillian.

"I'm Benny, what's your name?" asked Benny.

"Miss Rogers," said Lillian.

"Come off it," said Benny. "I mean your first name."

"Well—er—Lillian."

"I notice you haven't touched your drink, Lillian," said Benny.

"I don't drink, thank you," said Lillian.

"You should," said Benny. "It's part of the tour." He looked at Mr. Luften. "Isn't that right? One free drink in every club? Isn't that included in the cost of the tour?"

Mr. Luften didn't bother to answer. He turned his head away.

"If you want the drink you may have it," said Lillian. "Thanks," said Benny. He wolfed it down.

Lillian turned to Connie. "Now don't you see you better continue on with us instead of remaining in this place?" Connie could see that she was shocked.

"What's wrong with this place?" asked Benny. "You won't hear better jazz anywhere in Paris."

Mr. Luften stood up. He was visibly upset. He was used to having members of his tour follow unquestioningly wherever he led them. "It's time for us to move on." He looked at Connie. "All of us."

They all stood up except Connie.

"If Connie stays," said Lillian, "then I stay, too." And she sat down again.

"Actually," said Mr. Luften, "the clubs we visit get progressively better." He looked at Eddie. "We've started with the poorest one." He turned to Connie and Lillian. "But if you two want to spend your entire evening here, I suppose there's nothing I can do about it."

"I'm not going to let Connie stay here alone," said Lillian.

"This is getting embarrassing," said Connie.

"Don't you want me to stay?" asked Lillian.

"Hang around," said Benny. "The evening's young." He nudged Lillian suggestively with his elbow. "Maybe later we'll cut out and I'll show you some places you'd never get to with Cook's Tours here."

"It's not right that Connie should stay here alone," said Lillian. "I'll have to remain, too."

"Don't stay here on my account," said Connie.

"Don't you want me to stay?" asked Lillian.

"Do whatever you want to do," replied Connie.

"She's staying," said Benny. He put his arm around her. She immediately removed it, holding his hand with the tips of her fingers as if it were a live lobster.

"Come on, girls," said Mr. Luften. The other two teachers followed him out.

Eddie smiled at Connie. "You upset him. He commands and the tourists are supposed to follow like trained puppies. I've seen him here before."

Benny caught the eye of a waiter and pantomimed taking a drink. The waiter nodded understandingly and took off.

Benny leaned behind Connie's back and whispered to Eddie, "Don't worry about the old crone. I'll run interference for you."

Connie overheard and resented Benny's suggestion. She also resented Lillian's being referred to as an old crone. Lillian was old and crotchety, but she was also one of the few people she had ever known who was completely devoid of prejudice toward Negroes or even self-consciousness in their presence. For this reason Connie couldn't stand anyone speaking slightingly about Lillian, even though she knew how easily Lillian could get on people's nerves. Still, she decided to hold her tongue and not make an issue out of Benny's remark.

"How do you like Paris?" Benny asked Lillian.

"Well," said Lillian, "I'd like it better if I felt better."

"What are wrong?" asked Benny. "What are wrong?"

Lillian's face screwed up as though she couldn't believe her ears. *"What are wrong?"* she repeated.

"Yeah," said Benny, "what are wrong?"

"What kind of English is that?" asked Lillian.

"Lillian happens to be an English teacher," said Connie.

"There's nothing wrong with 'what are wrong,' " said Benny. "I use the plural because you got to admit there's usually more than one thing wrong. Therefore people should say 'what are wrong' instead of 'what is wrong.' "

"Are you serious?" asked Lillian.

"I'm just *kibbitzing*," said Benny.

"You're what?" asked Lillian.

Connie laughed. "It means he's kidding you," she said.

"Ah, a *landsmann!*" exclaimed Benny.

"I know what that word means anyway," said Connie.

The waiter appeared with a bottle of champagne.

"Anyway," said Benny, "whatever it is that ails you, this will fix it up."

The waiter held the bottle up so that Benny could read its label. "Good year!" he said to the waiter. Then he hunched over the table and said to the others, "Think I know the difference?" He shrugged his shoulders to imply that he didn't.

"One of the girls said I should drink lots of Perrier Mineral Water," said Lillian. "It's supposed to be very good for the stomach."

"This is the same thing," said Benny. "Except it's got more bubbles."

"I know champagne when I see it," said Lillian.

"Who said otherwise?" asked Benny. "We know you're no square."

The bottle popped loudly when opened and the waiter filled their glasses.

"To a wonderful evening for all!" toasted Benny.

Lillian didn't touch her glass.

"Come on," said Benny, "be a sport."

"A little won't hurt you," said Connie.

Lillian sipped some.

As Connie glanced around, scrutinizing the faces of the people seated around her, she saw Marie sweep into the room. What a striking woman, she thought.

Marie looked around, smiled at some people she knew, looked at Eddie, who had his back to her, stared poker faced for a moment at Connie, and finally disappeared through the side door through which she had a moment earlier entered.

"Interesting-looking woman," Connie commented.

"Who?" asked Eddie.

"A very elegantly dressed woman," said Connie. "Colored. She came through that side door, looked around and shot out again."

"Must've been Marie," said Benny.

"Yeah," said Eddie.

They sat a while and then Benny said, "We've got to make a little more music now but don't you go away. We'll be back." He drank his glass of champagne and he and Eddie returned to the bandstand. The other musicians returned and they started playing another set.

"He drinks an awful lot," said Lillian. "And that man you know, the leader of the band, is awfully quiet, isn't he? You never know about these jazz musicians. They all drink and take dope."

"Oh, Lillian, don't be silly!" said Connie.

"They do, it's a fact!" Lillian insisted. "I read about it."

More people began coming into the place, French people. Connie was glad that there seemed to be no other American tourists.

"How long do you plan to stay?" asked Lillian.

"Until twelve-thirty."

"Goodness! That late?"

"And then we're going out. Eddie promised to show me the *real* Paris—*his* Paris."

"You're not serious?"

"I certainly am."

"What time will you get in?"

"I don't know. Mrs. Vogel has nothing planned for tomorrow. I'll be able to sleep late."

Lillian looked worried. "What's going to happen to *me?*"

Connie was tired of playing constant companion to Lillian. This was a good time to establish that she had no intention of doing it for the rest of their trip.

"Take a cab back to the hotel whenever you want to," said Connie.

She saw the frightened and perturbed expression on Lillian's face and felt sorry for her. "I'll take you back to the hotel if you want me to," she said.

"And then?"

"I'll come back here."

Lillian took another sip of champagne.

Connie realized that this was the first evening on the trip that she was away from the protection of her group of fellow-teachers, away from the watchful eye of Mrs. Vogel, away from the annoying presence of Mr. Luften. It felt wonderful. If she could ever save up enough money to go to Europe again it would never be with another tour.

After Eddie and Benny finished the set they rejoined Connie and Lillian at their table. Eddie didn't say much, and Connie wondered whether he was now sorry he had promised to take her out later. She felt perhaps she had better give him an opportunity to back out of his commitment; it might be the wise thing to do, especially with Lillian as upset as she was.

"I think I may take a rain check on your kind offer to show me around," she said.

She knew that if Eddie had any sensitivity at all he would be able to tell that she really didn't mean it, that she would prefer going out with him later. "It may be too late for us," she added.

"What are you talking about?" asked Benny. "The tour the creep is taking you two friends on won't end until three in the morning. You would've gotten in late if you had gone with them. What's the big rush to get home?"

"I'll take you out," said Eddie. "It'll be all right."

"Saturday night's the big night here," said Benny, "just like in New York."

Connie looked at Benny, then at Lillian.

"Don't worry about your pal," said Benny. "I'll take care of her. I'll see that she gets home safe and sound—after we rip up Paris a little." He laughed and poured himself another glass of champagne.

Connie saw the look of horror that came into Lillian's eyes. She turned to Eddie. "All right," she said. "If Lillian doesn't mind . . . .."

It was obvious that Lillian did mind but now Connie saw that Eddie was definitely sincere about wanting to take her out and this was more important to her than anything else.

At twelve-thirty Eddie came back to their table.

"Let's go," he said.

"Perhaps we can drop Lillian off at the hotel first," said Connie.

"If it wouldn't be too much trouble," said Lillian, hopefully. She started to stand up but Benny pulled her back down.

"Not on your life!" Benny said. "We've just met!" He took her hand and held it tightly.

Connie let Eddie steer her to the door. She knew that she shouldn't leave Lillian but here she was doing it and, to tell the truth, she didn't particularly care.

« 7 »

TRY TO do someone a favor, thought Lillian, and look what happens! No appreciation. Off she goes, leaving me stranded high and dry. How in the world will I ever get out of this? How will I get home? She nervously ran her hand back and forth over a wrinkle in the checkered tablecloth.

She sat alone at the table. Benny had gone back on the stand to play. Marie's Cave was more crowded now and the band was beginning to play louder and livelier.

Lillian had never gone to a nightclub back in the States. She had never had any interest in going. What a time to start, at her age, and in Paris!

She thought of picking herself up and darting out while Benny was still on the stand. But she couldn't bear the thought of walking alone past the dozen or so tables that stood between her and the door.

The waiter filled her glass with what was left in the bottle of champagne.

"Merci beaucoup, monsieur," she said, careful with the accent.

The waiter acknowledged her attempt with a condescending smile.

She listened to the couples at the nearby tables chatting away in French. The tables were crowded close together and she could hear their occupants talking. She thought that certainly after a year of the Berlitz Self-Teacher and the Linguaphone Records she would at least know conversational French. But here in Paris she couldn't understand a word of what they were saying.

At least Benny spoke English, he was an American. Peculiar fellow. Of course, he didn't mean those silly, flattering things he said. Goodness, he was considerably younger than she was. He couldn't be more than forty five. He was shorter than she and a bit on the obese side but otherwise pleasant-looking enough.

Naturally he didn't mean a word of what he said. He was trying to help out his friend Eddie, to keep her occupied so that Eddie would be able to step out with Connie, that was all there was to it. She wasn't born yesterday.

She was greatly surprised that Connie had gone off with Eddie. She recalled a movie she had seen with Katharine Hepburn in which Miss Hepburn had a romantic liaison with an Italian. But he was so handsome, and an *Italian*. Eddie was just an American jazz musician.

She took a sip of champagne. She felt a little heady. She didn't know whether it was the champagne or the stuffy atmosphere or the loud music or a little of each.

It was a lucky thing there were no planned activities for Sunday. She would be able to sleep late—if she could get to sleep. She hadn't had a good night's sleep since her first night aboard ship. And her stomach! It was nerves, that's probably what it was.

She had been so undecided about the trip. True, all her life she had planned on seeing Europe. She couldn't go during the war and she felt she should wait at least five years after the war for conditions to improve. Then five years after the war she suddenly felt afraid and, what was worse, a little too old.

She knew all along that she had been looking forward to Europe for more than its culture, its museums and historical landmarks. She had hoped to find in Europe what she had never found at home—romance. Perhaps even on the boat going over to Europe. Oh, not with a European necessarily. It could be with a fellow-teacher, a man who, like her, wouldn't know how to dance. They'd sit for long hours on their deck chairs under the moonlight and stars talking literature and poetry and philosophy, and then one night, say about the third night out, he'd hold her hand and they'd both know they were in love. Of course they'd be inseparable on the tour and the other teachers would gossip about them. *Look at them, they're always together,* they'd say, and laughingly refer to them as the lovebirds, but they wouldn't care, they wouldn't care about anything except each other. And then one night they'd announce their engagement and the other teachers would throw them a surprise party in Paris. They would wait, of course, until they got back to the States to get married—she owed that to her mother and sister. It would be a simple wedding. His parents would come and everyone would comment on how nice he and his folks were. He would teach in New York, and after the wedding she would give up her job and find a job teaching there. Perhaps he wouldn't teach in a public school, but rather in a college or university. Perhaps Columbia. The very next summer they'd go back to Europe again, only this time they would be together in the same cabin.

This was her dream. And then, one day, she realized that it was past happening. And the desire to go to Europe was no longer there.

Then her mother died and her sister asked her to move in with her and her husband. Their children were all married, some with grown children of their own, and they had the big house to themselves. It was pleasant for a while, and comfortable, and her sister and brother-in-law couldn't have been kinder to her. They were older than Lillian, neither of them worked, and one night as they sat eating their dinner and listening to Lillian recount what had happened in school that day Lillian realized (while she was talking to them the thought came to her) that she, like them, despite her teaching, was doing nothing but waiting to die.

She continued talking, telling them an amusing anecdote about a note little Tommy had brought from his mother asking that he be excused from the gymnasium class because she suspected he was allergic to basketballs, but all the while she kept thinking oh no, she wasn't old enough to wait around to die, sixty wasn't that old. And that evening she sent away the letter to Teachers Tours, Inc. inquiring about their special European trip for teachers she had seen advertised in the Sunday newspaper.

Her sister, all her friends, had encouraged her to take the trip. At first the idea thrilled her. The day her reservation was confirmed was a joyous occasion. But as the dateline for departure approached she grew frightened. She had planned well; studied French and Italian;

read over a dozen guidebooks; taken injections against typhoid, tetanus, and cholera; memorized eight foreign currency equivalents of the dollar; and outfitted herself with a complete nylon-dacron travel-light wardrobe, a dozen cakes of Palmolive soap, a half-dozen boxes of Kleenex, a half-dozen rolls of Scott's toilet paper, and a bottle of Lysol poured into an unbreakable plastic travel container.

Still she knew she was missing something terribly important. She and her sister checked and double-checked everything, and she knew that her sister spoke the truth when she said that the only thing she was missing was her confidence.

The night before leaving for New York she lay awake knowing full well that if it weren't for the embarrassment of having to face her sister and friends she'd cancel the trip.

Even meeting the other teachers, seeing how anxious and fearful some of them were, didn't make her feel any better. How she wished she could feel like those teachers who were obviously thrilled and excited to be going to Europe. She tried not to reveal the terror in her heart when the steward sounded the all-ashore-that's-going-ashore gong and her sister kissed her good-by.

She remained on deck together with the other teachers and watched as the boat moved slowly down the Hudson, past the Statue of Liberty, past the parachute jump at Coney Island. When the call for lunch sounded she went down to the dining room with the others and when she came up afterward it was cloudy and unclear and she could no longer see any land.

And now here she was—Paris! She knew it was too late for romance. In fact the only male teacher in the group was the very young and very unhappy-looking Mr. Weiner.

"Have you been behaving?" The words interrupted her reverie.

She noticed the band had stopped playing, but she hadn't noticed Benny come back to the table. He sat down and offered her a cigarette.

"I don't smoke, thank you."

"I guess one vice is enough for you," he said, pointing to her empty champagne glass.

"I've never drunk this much," she said. "I usually don't drink at all."

"No excuses, no excuses!" He signaled to the waiter. "I'll get that filled up again right away."

She knew the words she should say: "Please don't bother. I've had quite enough, thank you! I must go now." And following that she should rise and walk out.

Instead she said, "Do you play classical music, too?" And she moved her chair closer to the table.

"I used to when I was a kid," said Benny.

"Why did you give it up?"

"I got interested in jazz."

"Don't you like classical music?"

"Oh, I like it all right," said Benny. "I got nothing against it. It's just that it's not for me. I just don't dig long hair, if you know what I mean."

He waved hello to some people he knew at another table.

"Is this your first trip over here?" he asked.

"Yes."

"Why'd you wait so long?"

She noticed that now that Connie and Eddie were no longer present Benny had adopted a more serious tone.

"I think I better be getting back to the hotel," she said.

"What for? The evening's young. I told you I'd show you the sights."

"You don't have to."

"Don't be silly. It'll be my pleasure, my pleasure!"

The waiter approached with the bottle of champagne but suddenly stepped backward quickly to get out of the way of Marie, who had just come over.

"Where's Eddie?" Marie asked.

"He stepped out," replied Benny.

"Will he be back?"

"I don't think so."

Lillian sensed that Marie was disturbed. She herself was a little annoyed that Benny didn't bother to introduce her to this woman. Normally Lillian was quite bashful about meeting people but she knew that now she wouldn't mind at all, especially since the woman looked so interesting.

"Do you know where he went?" asked Marie.

"He went out with my friend," said Lillian. She knew that she shouldn't have said this. Eddie was an employee here and perhaps it wasn't right for him to have left this early. She knew it might be a tactless, troublemaking thing for her to have said but she resented being ignored by these two people and wanted to speak up and say something.

"The same girl who was sitting next to him before?" asked Marie.

"That's right," said Benny.

Lillian nodded her head.

"I guess he felt it was going to be quiet tonight," said Benny.

"Saturday night?" said Marie. "He knows that's always our busiest night. I'm surprised at him." She moved off to chat with some people at the tables. The waiter stepped forward and opened the champagne.

"Who's she?" asked Lillian.

"The Marie of Marie's Cave—the boss."

"She is very beautiful."

Benny shrugged his shoulders.

"Perhaps I shouldn't have said that he went out with Connie," said Lillian.

"Don't be silly," Benny said. "He doesn't have to account to her for everything he does."

"But he left so early."

"Big deal! There are nothing wrong, believe me, there are nothing wrong. Drink up."

But Lillian saw that Benny was troubled and knew that something was wrong. She took another sip of champagne.

She felt afraid but she also felt free. For the first time that she could remember she was alone and on her own. There had always been someone to tell her what to do. At home her family—her mother, her sister. At school the department heads, the supervisors, the principals. Even in going to Europe she had chosen to go with a tour of teachers, Mrs. Vogel, chaperon and guide.

There was no one now at Marie's Cave to tell her what to do. It felt good.

She hoped that Benny would stick to his promise to take her out afterward. You live only once.

« 8 »

THEIR CAB pulled up to the hotel. Connie knew that she should tell Eddie that he didn't have to accompany her inside, that he should remain in the cab and take it back to his place. Instead she said nothing when Eddie paid the driver and took her by the arm and escorted her into the hotel. Surely here she should say good night to him, make it plain that she didn't want him to come up to her room; there was really no point to it, anyway, since Lillian was there. But she said nothing. She wanted to be with him as long as possible.

As they passed by the desk Connie glanced at the concierge and thought she detected a mischievous smile.

The staircase to her floor was narrow and circular. Connie went ahead of Eddie. She tried not to wriggle as she walked, conscious that his eyes were on her. When they reached her floor Eddie walked beside her as she slowly led him toward her door.

The hotel was old but it stood up well. She had noticed how well preserved were so many of the old buildings in Paris. In the States, buildings were hardly ever kept up once they grew old or out of fashion.

Connie checked the number on the door to make sure that she was at the right room.

"Good night," she said.

"Aren't you going to invite me in?"

"It's five o'clock in the morning."

Eddie shrugged his shoulders as if to say so what.

"I'm exhausted," explained Connie, actually not feeling tired at all. "We've been to so many places . . . and it's so late."

Eddie didn't look convinced.

"And, besides, Lillian is inside."

Eddie looked puzzled.

"Teachers can't afford private rooms," said Connie. "I'm lucky just bunking with Lillian. Some of the girls sleep three and four in a room."

"Suppose there weren't any Lillian. Would you invite me in?"

"I don't know," said Connie. "I—I don't think so."

"What are you doing tomorrow?" asked Eddie.

"Are you kidding? I'm going to sleep!"

"I'm not doing anything tomorrow. I could show you around."

"You must be tired of showing me around by now."

"I've just shown you a little of Paris at night. There's also Paris by day—especially on a Sunday."

"I would like to hear Mass at Notre-Dame."

"Are you a Catholic?"

"No, but I thought it might be interesting."

"I've never been in Notre-Dame," he said.

"Why?"

"I don't know. Maybe it's like the New Yorker who's never been to the Statue of Liberty."

"But you're not a Frenchman," said Connie.

"I'll tell you what," said Eddie. "I'll make a deal with you. I'll go to Notre-Dame if you go with me."

"Fine," said Connie. "But let's not make it too early."

"About noon?"

"That won't give me much sleep."

"When you sleep you're dead to the world," said Eddie. "There are some other places I want to show you besides Notre-Dame."

"All right—noon, then."

He put his arms around her and kissed her. She didn't expect it, didn't move away and didn't kiss back.

"I'm sorry," he said. He had a look of being hurt and she felt sorry for him.

"I'm—I'm just tired, that's all," she said. "Here . . ." She put her arms around him, pressed her body against his and opened her lips as she kissed him.

"I'll see you tomorrow," he said. "Have you got the key to your room?"

She opened her bag and showed it to him. He smiled and walked down the corridor to the staircase. It was the first time she had seen him smile that way all evening.

She opened the door to her room as quietly as she could and tiptoed in. The room was dark but she didn't want to turn on the light for fear of waking Lillian.

She started to get undressed and, as her eyes became accustomed to the dark, she suddenly realized that Lillian's bed was empty. She turned on the light and looked at her watch. It was five-fifteen in the morning and Lillian wasn't back yet!

Could something have happened to her? She shouldn't have left her alone in the nightclub! Where could she be at this hour? Was she wandering around Paris lost? Or perhaps waylaid by a robber? What would a robber want with a poor old-maid schoolteacher? Where could she be?

She got undressed and went down the hall to the bath room. If it had been anyone but Lillian she wouldn't have worried. But she knew Lillian wasn't the type to gallivant around Paris at five in the morning.

She went back to her room and still no Lillian. She turned out the light and got into bed. One teacher missing. Maybe she was out with that other musician, Benny. Maybe Benny took her home and she went to bed with him. Good God, not Lillian. What would Mrs. Vogel and the others say in the morning if Lillian was still missing by then?

Oh well, there was no point in getting upset and worrying. It wouldn't help. The chances were that if anything dreadful had happened they'd hear about it soon enough. The chances were nothing dreadful had happened. But what could Lillian have been doing all this time?

She thought of the fascinating evening she had spent with Eddie. What a relief it was to be able to visit places without being herded around as she was on the tours. Eddie had taken her to so many places.

There was Les Halles, a market district that came alive when the rest of Paris went to sleep, a huge place where fruits and vegetables arrived from the farms, buzzing with workmen unloading and uncrating, redolent with the sweet smell of fresh produce.

In Les Halles they had gone to a restaurant crowded with French workmen, mainly butchers. The work-aprons the butchers wore were covered with animal blood, but she wasn't bothered by it. It was all part of the atmosphere. The workmen laughed, joked and shouted to one another as they drank their wine and ate their food and she wondered why more Frenchmen couldn't be so jolly.

But the main attraction in Les Halles, the main interest, as everywhere they had gone that evening, was still Eddie. She had never known anyone like him. It wasn't only that he was terribly handsome; he was subdued in manner, but everything about him was electrically alive. She felt he wasn't just a talker, as so many were with whom she had gone out, full of wonderful ideas frustrated by the circumstances of their drearily dull lives. Eddie was a man of action, perhaps wrong action, escapist action, but at least action. And if some of the things he did were wrong they could just as easily be right, for *at least he did things.*

And she could see that he was respected. Everywhere they went people greeted him exuberantly. She hadn't imagined Eddie was the celebrity he turned out to be.

Wherever he took her, the boîtes, cafés, little out-of-the-way places, they were welcomed. It seemed they could go anywhere in Paris without having to worry or even be conscious of the fact that they were Negroes.

It was different from the States. Pleasantville, Louisiana, was a Jim Crow town. Chicago was a fairly liberal city but there were still some places there that she would hesitate to go to. Here it was different. Nobody cared about the color of your skin.

She had enjoyed most of the places to which Eddie had taken her; mainly, she knew, because it was just being with Eddie.

There was one café, however, where she had felt rather uncomfortable. It was in Montmartre. For one thing it was embarrassing when she walked in with Eddie and the master of ceremonies pointed to them, said a few words she couldn't understand, and everybody started laughing at them. When they sat down the master of ceremonies pointed to them again, added a few more remarks, and there was another burst of derisive-sounding laughter. Eddie's explanation that it was the custom here to poke fun at the customers didn't make her feel any better.

"In this café nothing is sacred," Eddie said. "There are quite a few places like this in Paris. Not only do they poke fun at the customers, but at everything. They say things about their government that Americans would never say about the United States."

"Maybe that's because they don't have to," Connie answered.

"Come off it," said Eddie. "You have to admit there's no freedom any more back in the States."

"I don't have to admit anything of the kind," said Connie. "There's been a loss of freedom, yes, but I wouldn't say there's no freedom."

He didn't seem to want to start an argument with her and abruptly changed the topic. He started telling her about the gimmicks some of the other nightclubs had, describing one Left Bank club where the customers were requested to smash their plates on the floor.

While she hadn't enjoyed the cabaret in Montmartre she did enjoy Montmartre itself. True, it was overcrowded with tourists, but she liked its narrow, hilly, winding streets, and she liked seeing the Sacré-Coeur Church. And Eddie took her to a little side street where she got a magnificent view of the brilliantly lighted city below.

But she supposed that what she would remember more than anything else that evening was the party Eddie had taken her to. Almost everyone there was an American expatriate, and they made her feel completely out of place.

The apartment where the party was held was overcrowded and hot. At one point she had mentioned how hot it was to a man seated next to her. He replied, "But, my dear, it's warmth from Paris—the womb of the world!"

When she told a bohemian-looking girl that she was going to Spain as part of her tour the girl said, "Aren't you lucky! The bullfights! Bullfighting is the most beautiful experience I know. It's poetry, sheer poetry."

"I don't even know if I'll go to one," said Connie. "I suppose I'll have to but I know I won't like it. I just can't stand the thought of seeing an animal killed before my very eyes."

"But you don't understand," said the bohemian-looking girl, "that bullfighting is the dramatic quintessence of ego versus id, of life instinct versus death instinct!"

Connie didn't understand. Nor did she understand the need for the loud obscene remarks that were hurled about with such abandon.

"It's just in the two most important areas of life that I would rate America a zero—food and fucking!" This shouted by a tall, lanky lad whose curly blond hair reminded Connie of Shirley Temple's.

No, she hadn't been comfortable at the party. She did not really dislike the people there. Rather, she felt terribly sorry for them. They were pathetic souls. They were neither Frenchmen nor Americans, certainly more American than French though they might not care to admit it, and their boisterous bitterness was only the obvious disguise for feelings of isolation and inadequacy.

What she had enjoyed most during the evening was just walking along the Seine on the little path that paralleled the river. It was dark and quiet and peaceful. They hardly talked. There were other strollers, mostly young lovers, and under some of the bridges slept old men raggedly dressed. Once in a while a barge moved slowly down the river. Once they passed the spot where the sightseeing boats were tied up alongside the dock. Yes, this had been the best part of the evening.

Connie heard a key in the latch. The door slowly opened and Lillian walked in. Connie sat up.

"Where have you been all this time?"

"Oh, Connie," said Lillian, "it was awful." Lillian snapped on the light. Connie blinked her eyes. "The places that man took me to! They're too shocking to talk about! I'll never get over it! I've never had such a miserable time in my life!"

The sudden light made it difficult for Connie to get a good look at Lillian. But she could see her well enough to know that she had never looked happier or more alive.

Connie didn't have to ask what had happened. Lillian couldn't contain herself. She began to talk. Talk? It wasn't talk. It was a pouring out, a gushing forth, a firehose going full blast. There was no stopping her. It was amazing that words spoken that fast could be understood.

"First Benny decided that we should get something to eat. We went to a restaurant. From the outside it looked lovely, very elegant, in fact. The people inside were all dressed very well. They looked quite wealthy, as a matter of fact. We sat down and then I noticed the murals on the wall. They were obscene, positively obscene, that's the only word I can use to describe them."

Of course, with Lillian, thought Connie, it was hard to know whether something was really obscene or the mildest form of Rabelaisian humor.

"They showed men and women doing the most outrageous things! Then the waiter brought the rolls over and, I know you won't believe this, I know I wouldn't if anyone told it to me, but I saw it with my own two eyes: the rolls—how can I explain it—they were baked in the shape of genitals—male genitals! The food was served in chamber pots . . ."

It was obscene, Connie decided.

". . . and a little lamb wandered around from table to table drinking wine the people served it! When I told Benny how revolting I thought the place was he pointed to all the photographs on the walls of famous men who had dined there, including a signed photograph of Albert Schweitzer! Do you really believe Albert Schweitzer could have gone to a place like that?"

"Good for him if he did," said Connie.

"Anyway, the worst thing was when the host went around and made all the women stand on top of the table while he lifted their skirts all the way up and put a garter around their thighs."

Lillian opened her purse and took out the garter. "He put one around my leg, too, only I took it off when we went swimming!"

"Swimming!" exclaimed Connie.

"Next we went to a nightclub in the Place Pigalle. It looked horrible from the outside and I didn't want to go in, believe me. There were pictures on the outside of women with practically no clothes on and that's exactly how they were on the inside. I've never see anything like it in all my life. And Benny, wouldn't you know that he'd get a table in the very first row. I was never so embarrassed. The girls had absolutely nothing on but little silver things to cover their private parts and I don't know how they stayed on. I mean there were no strings or anything attached to hold them in place."

"So you saw a real French girlie show," said Connie. "That's more than the rest of us have done."

"We were so close that their derrières were practically in our faces. If I had just held out my hand I could have touched them. Champagne came with the table and Benny insisted I keep drinking it. Oh, it was horrible! I was beginning to feel dizzy. And then the next thing I knew I was in another one of those dreadful places, except here I know I'll never forget this for the rest of my life—the women, with all their scanty clothes on, were men! They had shapely legs like a woman . . .

and faces with make-up on, but they were men! And don't ask me how I know!"

Connie was reminded of a nightclub she had been taken to once in Chicago where the entertainment consisted of this type of female impersonation. She could imagine the effect a French version of this must have had on Lillian.

"The place was hot and noisy and sticky and when I told Benny I just had to get some fresh air he asked me if I knew how to swim. I didn't know what he was driving at so I said yes. As a matter of fact, I've always been a good swimmer and I told him how during the war I used to teach army nurses how to swim. So he said fine, we were going swimming. I told him that there couldn't be a pool open this late at night, or rather early in the morning, but he assured me that there was. I told him I didn't like the idea of wearing public bathing suits but he told me not to worry about it and when we got there I saw that the men and women got undressed in the same locker room.

"Believe me, I didn't want to go through with it, I wanted to run out, but he forced me. He's a regular monster, Benny. And to think he's not even a Frenchman, but an American! Oh, I can't bear to bring myself to tell you about it! He forced me to strip! Yes, that's just what he did. And in front of all of those other people! It was a regular nudist club. And when he dragged me inside into the pool I saw that everybody there was swimming with no clothes on at all. Not a stitch! And, worst of all, I was naked myself! And so was Benny! I could see everything!

"To get away from him I held my nose and jumped into the water and swam to the other side of the pool. Benny jumped into the water, too, and immediately began cavorting with some young naked thing who was there. She swam doing the backstroke and he swam doing the crawl right on top of her. 'Look at us! he screamed.' Like at the Aquacade at the World's Fair in New York. She's Eleanor Holm and I'm Johnny Weissmuller!

"All the people in the pool started applauding and screaming 'Bravo!' Then he began showing off—swimming by himself as fast as he could. He was a very good swimmer, I must admit. He said he had learned how at Coney Island.

"Finally we got out and got dressed and he took me home in a taxicab. I didn't say a word to him all the way home. I've been hoping that this is all a horrible dream but I know it isn't because I can still smell the chlorine."

She raised her wrist to her nose and sniffed. "I can still smell the chlorine."

Connie didn't know whether to laugh or cry, to feel sorry for Lillian or glad.

"Go to sleep," said Connie. "Maybe we'll both wake up in the morning and find it's all been a dream."

Quickly, silently, unsteadily Lillian got undressed. Connie stretched out under the covers, watching her.

Lillian stood in the middle of the room naked. This was the first time Connie had seen her without any clothes. She was usually extremely modest about her body. She put on her slippers, took her toilet kit and a towel and opened the door.

"Lillian!" cautioned Connie. "Put on a robe!"

"Oh yes," said Lillian. She put her things down, went to the closet, opened it, then seemed to change her mind and closed it again.

"I'm so tired," she said. She crossed to her bed and stretched out on top of the covers.

"Lillian!" called Connie. "Lillian!"

But the regular breathing of sleep was all she heard in reply. She slipped out of her own bed and went to Lillian's. She wondered if she should try to get Lillian into her pajamas, and decided against it. She had to smile to herself as she managed to get Lillian's blanket out from under her and cover her with it, arranging her head comfortably on the pillow. Then she went back to her own bed and fell asleep.

《 9 》

EDDIE'S NOT-quite-peaceful sleep was interrupted by the persistent ringing of the doorbell. He looked at the clock on top of the dresser. The room was darkened by the drawn blinds and he had to strain to see. It was nine thirty in the morning. He dragged himself from the bed and opened the door.

It was Benny. He looked bleary-eyed and unshaven and obviously hadn't been to bed all night. He walked into the room and sat wearily down in a chair.

"Anything wrong?" asked Eddie.

"No," Benny said. "I just dropped by to say hello."

"At nine-thirty in the morning?"

Benny saw Eddie's English cigarettes lying on the night table alongside the bed. He took one and lit it. "You're the one who's always saying how when a guy sleeps he's dead to the world. You're always saying we really don't need as much sleep as we get."

"But this is Sunday morning," said Eddie. "I didn't get in until a little while ago."

"That schoolteacher chick?"

Eddie nodded.

"Nice girl?"

"She's all right."

"I'm sorry if I woke you," said Benny.

"Well, I was going to get up in a little while anyway. I have a date at twelve."

"I feel lousy," said Benny.

"What happened?"

Benny put the cigarette in the ashtray and nervously rubbed his hands together. "I did a lousy thing last night. The old biddie—you know, the chick's roommate I took care of for you—I made her go out with me. Sort of a practical joke. She looked so prim and prissy I just couldn't resist trying to shock her. I took her to some skin joints and then over the Piscine des Naturistes. I made her get undressed and jump in the pool naked. I think I must've shocked her something awful."

Eddie smiled. The picture of the old lady in the pool naked was funny. "She'll get over it," said Eddie. "But why'd you do it?"

"I told you," said Benny. "I wanted to shock her. I guess I wanted to hurt her. I realized that later, I guess, after I got back to my hotel. I was so sore at myself for wanting to hurt her that I couldn't sleep. I sat up trying to figure it out. Now why would I want to do a thing like that? Hurt a poor little old defenseless lady?" He shook his head as he thought about it.

Eddie put on a robe and shuffled into the kitchen. There were some croissants in the bread basket. He started to heat some water. Benny continued talking from the other room.

"You know how I feel about all the jerks who are always blasting our country. You know how it gripes me and I always put them in their place. Usually they're guys who couldn't make it back in the States, so they come over here where it's easier to be a bum and they bitch all the time. It burns me up the way these guys talk and the way a lot of the Frenchmen are always making cracks about America, too. Well, you know, I think maybe the reason I feel so lousy about what I did last night is that I'm beginning to get like all the other guys; I'm beginning to take it out on America, too, and I was using what's-her-name Lillian as a scapegoat."

Eddie returned to the room with two cups and saucers. He put them down on a small coffee table. "You want some coffee, don't you?"

Benny didn't say anything.

"It'll be ready in a minute. Look, it probably wasn't as bad as you say it was. Maybe she even enjoyed it."

"I know she didn't," said Benny. "I was just being cruel to her. I guess I felt this way when I first saw her in the club. I guess I'm beginning to feel like the others—I don't like all the Americans coming over."

"Some of them are pretty bad," said Eddie.

"Yeah," said Benny. "Like the dumb drunk bastard the other night who wanted you to play *Melancholy Baby*."

"That's right," said Eddie.

Benny picked up his cigarette and took a long drag. "But they're not all like that," he said. "The old lady was a real hick but otherwise okay. I did it out of nastiness. It must've been terribly embarrassing for her."

"If you feel that way about it," said Eddie, "call her up and apologize."

"I wonder how I can get in touch with her, I don't even remember the name of her hotel. I don't even know her last name."

"I'll get you her number."

"You know it?"

"I'll get it for you."

"How?"

"I'm going to see Connie later."

"I'll go along with you," said Benny. "Then I can apologize to her in person."

"If you want to," said Eddie. "I still don't know why you're making such a fuss about it, though."

"Because I don't want to get like all those other phonies, hating America and Americans," shouted Benny. "I like America. And I like Americans, too."

"Why don't you go back?" asked Eddie.

"Now you know better than to ask a stupid question like that. You know how I feel about the music business back there."

"I'll get the coffee," said Eddie. He went back to the kitchen.

Benny rubbed his chin. "You got anything I can shave with?"

"The electric razor is in the bathroom."

Benny started for the bathroom, then changed his mind and went into the kitchen. "Go back to America? That's a helluva thing to say!"

Eddie picked up the plate of croissants and the coffee pot and carried them into the other room. Benny followed on his heels. Eddie poured the coffee.

"Go back to the way music is in the States," said Benny. "No, thank you! The stinking union, those murderous one-night stands traveling all over the country, the grubby managers interested only in the buck, the gangsters and vultures who want their boys to be coke-heads or hop-heads or mainliners or whiskey-heads or winos so they can keep them under their thumbs. Go back to that? No, thank you! Europe is the only place for me, man, the only place where I can play the kind of music I want to play and not the kind of music some greasy manager thinks will bring in the bucks."

"Maybe you ought to go back for a visit," said Eddie. "Might be good for you."

"Ah," said Benny, "I don't need it. I got nobody there anymore. If my mother and father were alive it would be a different story. Or if my aunt was alive. But when she died two years ago I felt there was nothing to make me want to go back again. Here I am forty-five, only forty-five, and so many of the people I knew are dead. Not only relatives but you'd be surprised how many of my friends I've heard have died. Why go back to the States? I'll live out the rest of my life here!" He broke a croissant in half and dipped it into the coffee.

"You're beginning to sound like an old man," said Eddie. "Maybe you ought to go back to the States for a while. Find yourself a wife there and bring her back to Paris."

Benny looked up from his coffee and stared at Eddie. "My aunt," he shouted explosively. "That's it, my aunt! That's why I felt so lousy about Lillian. My aunt never came over to Europe, but if she had why she'd be the same type of square like Lillian. I'd get furious if anyone pulled on my aunt what I pulled on Lillian. That's why I'm so upset. Now I realize it!"

"You'll apologize to her later and it'll all be straightened out," said Eddie.

"I've been hanging around too many of the gripers," said Benny. "That's my trouble. I'm getting to be just like them. It's no good."

"You haven't had a vacation in a long time, have you, Benny? A trip back to the States might be good for you."

"What's this bit about going back to the States? What are you pressing for? Maybe you're the one who wants to take a trip back!"

"Me? Are you kidding?" said Eddie. "What would I want to go back for?"

"I don't know, except you keep pushing it so hard for me."

Eddie finished his cup of coffee. "I'm still sleepy," he said. "I think I'm going to try to get some more shut-eye. Why don't you go back to your place to shave? Pick me up in an hour and a half, around eleven-thirty, and we'll go over to see the girls." He took off his robe and slipped back into bed.

"You mean you want me to leave?" asked Benny.

"If you want to sit here, sit here."

Benny looked at himself in the mirror. "I guess I look kind of messy. You got a shirt to lend me?"

"Sure. You know where they are."

"Do you think it's all right for me to go over with you?" asked Benny. "I mean maybe it will embarrass the old girl even more."

"It'll be all right."

"Maybe I shouldn't go. Maybe I should just call her up."

"Do what you want."

"I need a shave."

Eddie sat up. "For chrissake, Benny, let me get some sleep, will you! If you want to shave, shave! If you want to go back to your place, go back!" He put his head back on the pillow and closed his eyes but he knew it would be impossible to sleep with Benny in the same room, sitting there and talking to him.

He talked without opening his eyes. "Benny, go back to your place, huh? I'll see you later."

"You're turning me out just like I tossed out Michel."

"What's this about Michel?"

"Nothing," said Benny.

He heard Benny get up and leave the apartment, softly closing the door behind him.

He wondered what Benny had meant by that remark about Michel and he couldn't understand why Benny was so disturbed over having embarrassed the old lady. It probably wasn't as embarrassing to her as Benny felt. And why was Benny always so afraid that people might think he hated America? What made him so patriotic? He was a funny guy. Warm and friendly and happy-go-lucky on the surface. Always joking. But wearing his jokes as armor.

There was nothing wrong with Benny's coming along to apologize, just as long as he and Lillian didn't tag along with him and Connie afterward. He wanted to be alone with her. And he wanted to look good when he saw her. That was the real reason he'd gone back to bed to get another hour's rest.

Again he thought of what Benny had said about Michel. Something about tossing him out. Tossing him out of where?

The telephone rang. God damn it! Just as he was beginning to feel relaxed. He reached over and picked it up.

"Hello, Eddie, my friend, how are you?" The voice drawled a lazy French.

"My God, Michel, I was just thinking about you."

"How are you, Eddie?"

"I'm fine, thanks, Michel. How are you?"

"I'm not at home. Something terrible has happened."

"What? Look, if it's about the letters . . ."

"I'm in prison."

"What?"

"They will let me out, though, if you come down and sign a paper."

Eddie tossed his blanket aside and sat up on the edge of the bed. "What happened?"

"I can't tell you now. Can you come down right away?" He gave Eddie the address.

"Isn't there anyone else you can call?"

"You will be shocked when you see me. They gave me the treatment. My face is quite disfigured."

"Can't you call your brother? Can't he come down and get you?"

"Can't you come down, Eddie? They want me to stop talking now. I better go."

Eddie heard the phone click at the other end. He hung up and dropped back on the bed.

His irritation with Michel had passed into anger. Michel had been given everything—talent, the security of a good family, friends who respected him. Yet steadily, almost deliberately, he was throwing his advantages away. And now, Eddie thought, he calls on me to help him. Why me? Of all the people in Paris, why me?

But the answer lay already in his mind: *Because he knows I will.*

He got dressed and left for the police station.

《10》

THE DAY hadn't started right, Benny breaking in with his conscience showing, the phone call from Michel. Now the taxicab he was riding on his way to the police station stuck in a traffic jam.

"What's the matter, driver?" asked Eddie, impatiently, "Why all the traffic this time of the day?"

The driver shrugged his shoulders apathetically. He had a fare, the meter was running; they could be stuck here all morning for all he cared.

A gendarme strolled by, as apathetic as the driver.

Eddie stuck his head out of the window. "Officer . . ."

The gendarme came over to the taxicab and saluted.

"What's holding up the traffic?"

"There's some sort of Arab demonstration up ahead. They've blocked off the traffic for a few blocks." He waited to see if Eddie had any further questions, then slowly strolled ahead. It struck Eddie that he was in no great hurry to get to the scene of the trouble; let the special riot squads take care of it.

The taxi driver had suddenly become alive at the mention of the word "Arab." "I don't know about those Arabs," he said. "Of course, they're human beings like everyone else, but it is a fact that they cause nothing but trouble. Last week they had another demonstration. Do you think it was about the situation in Africa? No! It was about the situation right here in Paris! They say they're discriminated against."

"Don't worry about the Arab situation," said Eddie. "Worry about getting us out of here."

He opened the door of the car and looked ahead to see if the traffic had started to move. A North African peddler, taking advantage of the captive market, strolled down between the rows of automobiles, carrying rugs and furs.

"A nice fur piece for your girlfriend?" he asked Eddie.

"Beat it, you son-of-a-bitch!" yelled the taxi driver. "You scum, you swine!"

Placidly the peddler continued on his way, offering his wares without success.

"Take it easy," cautioned Eddie.

"Some of them have their nerve," said the driver. "The trouble they give us in the Colonies, and then they want to be admitted into the new public housing here in Paris. And they complain about being kept out of jobs and schools, too."

The traffic wasn't moving. Eddie reached into his pocket for his wallet. "I think I better get out here and get another taxi on the other avenue."

"Those Algerians," said the driver.

"Shut up!"

The driver turned around, startled. "What's wrong? I'm a fair man, a democratic man. France is a democratic country. We don't discriminate against Negroes, like they do in America. But these North Africans, these Algerians, with them it's a different story. They're not—"

"I said shut up!" He looked at the meter, took the sum from his wallet, threw the money in the driver's perplexed face and stormed out of the cab.

He rapidly walked a few blocks to where the traffic was moving and got another cab. He told the driver where he wanted to go.

"We'll have to go a roundabout route," said the driver. "There's some sort of Arab demonstration on ahead."

"I know," said Eddie.

"Those North Africans . . ."

"I don't want to hear a word about the North Africans!" snapped Eddie. "Just keep quiet and do your job."

The police station was an old stone fortress. Inside, the cavernous rooms contained only the most essential furniture—all of it ancient and in need of repair or replacement. In the main room, just off the entrance, three gendarmes and three clerks in civilian clothes worked on mountains of paper forms—sorting, initialing, filling-in and stamping, repeatedly stamping. On the desks were at least fifty different types of rubber stamps. Each time Eddie entered any public bureau he was conscious of an enormous amount of paperwork going on—tirelessly, endlessly and, he often suspected, needlessly.

A gendarme directed Eddie to a woman sitting in a wire booth, the inside walls of which were lined with a variety of multi-sized forms. Eddie explained his mission and the woman carefully took three different forms from the shelves and handed them to him. It took fifteen minutes for him to fill them out on a long table in the center of the room. He was then directed to an inquiry desk in another room. There Eddie learned that Michel was no longer in the police station.

"Has he been released?"

The stiff-necked police official examined closely Eddie's application of inquiry. He was a fleshy, pale-faced man and his jowls shook with even slight movements of his head. "You're not a relative?"

"No."

"We've managed to notify his relatives. I believe it was his brother we finally got in touch with. You must be the friend he called."

"That's right."

"You're an American?"

"Yes."

"He is a French Negro. A citizen of France."

"I know."

"He was born here. There aren't many like that. French Negroes actually born in Paris. Very interesting."

"Where is he?" asked Eddie, conscious that he was raising his voice.

The police official scribbled something on the form Eddie filled out. Without looking up, he replied, "He's been transferred to the hospital."

Eddie stared at the police official's fat, powerful hands. "He said that he was beaten. Did you beat him that badly that he had to be sent to the hospital? What did he do?"

"He was transferred to a hospital for mental disorders. I think it was either the Hôspital de Villejuif or the Aisle de Charenton. "He consulted an index file on his desk." It's the Aisle de Charenton. He is crazy, your friend."

"What happened?"

The police official smiled and tapped his right temple with his forefinger. "I told you. He is crazy."

A gendarme and a short Negro dressed meticulously in a black suit approached the desk. The short Negro carried light gray gloves, a black fedora and a malacca cane. Eddie had never seen the man before but he noticed a slight resemblance between him and Michel and assumed that he was Michel's brother. The gendarme who had escorted the little man into the room left.

"Monsieur Rabu?" asked the police official behind the desk.

"That's correct," answered the little man. "Now what has happened with my brother!"

He seemed to Eddie to be more annoyed than concerned.

"He was picked up this morning around the Place de L'Opéra for purse-snatching and resisting arrest."

"My God!" exclaimed the brother.

"The funny thing is he didn't try to run away."

"Then how can he be charged with resisting arrest?" asked Eddie.

The police official was plainly annoyed at Eddie's interference. "When he grabbed the purse and the lady started to scream he didn't run away," said the police official. "He opened her purse right on the spot and began rummaging through it. But when the gendarme came over and demanded to know what was going on, that's when he resisted arrest. In fact, he even struck the officer."

Eddie turned to the brother. "It sounds awfully fishy to me," he said. The brother looked at him disdainfully and then turned to the police official. "What else?" he asked, calmly but obviously seething at Eddie underneath.

"When we brought him in he gave us some cock-and-bull story about the lady having a letter for him from Stravinsky and not wishing to hand it over to him. Of course the lady had never seen him before and didn't know what he was talking about. Naturally she didn't even know Stravinsky. What a story! There's been an outbreak of purse-snatching recently in Paris and we thought this young man might be part of a ring we've been trying to track down. We soon found out he wasn't."

"But you tried to beat a confession out of him just the same," said Eddie.

"We have our regular methods," said the police official.

"I can't say I'm surprised," said the brother. "I knew he would come to no good."

"He's sick," said Eddie. "This obsession he has about getting letters of recommendation from famous people is part of it."

"He's been sick a long time," said the brother. "Ever since he started playing in nightclubs." He looked at Eddie hatefully. "You're one of those people, too, aren't you?"

"I'm a jazz musician, if that's what you mean," said Eddie. "And your brother is one of the greatest jazz musicians I know."

"Jazz is not music," insisted the brother. "It may mean something in the cultural desert of America but not over here. Like so many of your other exports it's a strictly inferior product."

"I didn't know he was a jazz musician," interjected the police official. "He said nothing about it. He said something about being a teacher, or wanting to be a teacher, and that was why he needed the letter from Stravinsky. But by that time we knew he was crazy and had him transferred to the Aisle de Charenton."

"If only he were a teacher," said the brother. "If only he hadn't got mixed up with you fellows and your jazz this wouldn't have happened to him." He addressed the police official. "Look at his family. His father a doctor, his sister a doctor, I'm in the diplomatic service, and he has to become a jazz musician. It's a disgrace!"

"Maybe your father or your sister ought to go to see him at the hospital," said Eddie. "If they are doctors they—"

"I'll attend to it," interrupted the brother.

"But he's sick," said Eddie.

"He is a crazy man," agreed the police official.

"When can I take him out of there?" asked the brother.

"You'll have to wait a few days," replied the police official. "Once he's admitted he has to remain there a few days for observation. Visiting hours are at two o'clock today."

"Perhaps I'll drop over to see him, too," said Eddie.

"You keep out of this," said the brother. "Your kind has caused him enough trouble."

The police official smiled at the hostility between the two men.

The brother looked at his watch. "I have an important appointment at two o'clock. I trust that there are visiting hours tomorrow?"

"Same time," answered the police official.

"Thank you," said the brother. Without bothering to glance at Eddie he turned on his heel and left the room. Eddie and the police official looked at one another.

"Diplomatic service!" commented the police official. "If he wanted to he could get his brother out of the hospital today."

"How did you come to realize that he was sick and not a purse snatcher?" asked Eddie.

"We have our methods. . . ."

"You mean you couldn't beat a confession out of him!"

"That's enough of that!" The police official was plainly angered by Eddie's having repeated the charge. He stood up. "You Americans think you can tell us how to do everything!"

"I've been here twelve years," said Eddie. "I'm more French than I am American."

"That's what you think," said the police official. "You may talk our language perfectly but you'll never be able to speak our language, if you know what I mean. Now leave me alone. I'm busy."

"Is there a telephone I can use?"

"Are you going to call the American Embassy?" He laughed. "It won't help. Your friend is a French citizen."

"Is there a phone I can use?"

The police official took up his pen and buried his face in his papers.

Eddie left the room. A gendarme in the corridor directed him to a public telephone. He called Benny.

"Where are you?" asked Benny. "I was just about to leave for your place."

He gave Benny the address of the hotel at which Connie and Lillian were staying. "I'll meet you there at twelve."

"But where are you?"

"I'll explain when I see you."

"I've some great news," said Benny. "Some of the boys have cooked up a shindig for Wild Man Moore tonight. We're both invited. A dinner at the Café Francis. Should be a helluva lot of fun. I've accepted for both of us."

"But I'll probably be busy tonight."

"You can bring the chick."

"We'll see. I'll see you over at their hotel."

"We should have a helluva lot of fun tonight with Wild Man Moore. He's a character."

"I'll see you later."

"They've been going crazy over him here. Hank Dixon called. He said that—"

"Benny, I can't talk to you on the phone now. I have to get going or I'll be late."

"Okay. See you later."

It was a few blocks from the police station to the taxi cab stand. Eddie walked them slowly.

He couldn't figure out what reason Michel had for his breakdown. He'd led the good life. It wasn't as though he'd been brought up in America where being colored meant that you were a second-class citizen. He had been born and brought up in France where it didn't make any difference. And his family had dough. He'd had all the opportunities in the world. What was his problem?

And what was the matter with Benny? Was everybody going nuts today?

❪ 11 ❫

THE LOBBY was crowded. Eddie noticed the two girls who had been with Connie and Lillian the night before in the club. They recognized him and he half-smiled at them in acknowledgment. Benny was slumped in a chair in the corner reading the Paris edition of the *Herald Tribune*. As Eddie approached, Benny looked up.

"Where were you?" asked Benny.

Eddie told him about Michel.

"That's terrible! I mean I knew that French cat was off his rocker but I never expected him to really flip. Why only the other day he bust in on me, and—"

"I ought to try to get to see him," said Eddie.

"Yeah. Maybe we'll go later, huh?"

"I'm going to be with the girl."

"Oh."

"And, by the way, I want to be with her alone."

Benny looked apprehensive. "I'm not going to run interference for you with Lillian again."

"Do what you want. Only I hope you weren't planning on tagging along with us."

"Don't be silly. I got plenty to do on my own."

"Okay," said Eddie. "Let's go."

They walked to the house phone. Connie answered almost the moment it rang and told Eddie to come up.

Eddie wished Benny weren't there. He wanted to be alone with Connie. He wanted to forget about Benny and Michel and being stuck

in a traffic jam on his way to see Michel. He wanted to forget about
Marie and her new boyfriend, and her plans to expand the club. He
wanted to stop thinking about everything except being alone with
Connie.

She opened the door, smiling cheerfully. The smile dropped.
"What's wrong?" she asked.

Eddie didn't understand what she meant. "You two look about as
happy as a pair of sick fish."

Eddie knew that he was never good at hiding the way he felt. He
felt lousy so he probably looked lousy. And Benny looked as though
he was all set to start wailing the blues.

"Well come on in," said Connie.

They entered and sat down. Connie sat on the edge of the bed.
Eddie tried to look more cheerful. He fought against sinking into one
of his quiet, brooding moods. Especially since he was going to spend
the day with Connie.

"Benny's feeling sad," said Eddie, "because of what happened last
night."

"Lillian told me all about it," said Connie.

Benny looked pained and put his hand to his forehead.

"It's not that bad," said Connie.

"Where is she now?" asked Eddie, wanting to get the thing over
with, wanting to get rid of Benny, wanting to be alone with Connie.
"Benny wants to apologize."

"Apologize? What for?" asked Connie. "I think she rather enjoyed
herself last night."

Benny took his hand away from his forehead. "Maybe she didn't
tell you everything."

"There couldn't have been more," said Connie.

Eddie took out his pack of cigarettes and started to take one. Connie crossed over to him and took one for herself. "Well, we know what's bothering Benny," she said, "but what's eating you?"

"Nothing. Nothing's eating me," said Eddie, not wanting to think about it, let alone talk about it. "Where's Lillian now?"

"Maybe she's at confession," said Benny.

They laughed.

"She's out walking it off, trying to clear her head."

"It must've been pretty bad," said Benny. "I mean, could she eat anything this morning?"

"Are you kidding? The breakfasts are prepaid. She wouldn't miss a meal if she had to take it intravenously."

"Do you think she'll be back soon?" asked Benny.

"She should be back in a few minutes."

"I'll wait for her. I just hope there are nothing wrong." He crossed his legs and put his hands on his knee. "It's all right if I wait for her here in the room, isn't it?"

"Why don't you wait for her downstairs in the lobby?" suggested Eddie. "She may not be coming back to the room."

"Oh, no," said Connie. "She said she'd be coming back here. It's all right if you wait here."

"Well there's no point in our waiting around," said Eddie. "Let's take off."

Connie agreed. She got her handbag. "Don't worry too much about Lillian," she said to Benny. "I'm sure she's not *too* mad at you."

Benny was too engrossed in his own thoughts to answer.

They walked down the stairs, through the lobby past the teachers, who smiled self-consciously at them, out into the street.

"Can we walk from here to Notre-Dame?" asked Connie. "It's such a beautiful day."

She wore a tweed suit, a green scarf, unfeminine walking shoes.

Eddie looked up at the glaring sun. "It's pretty hot for a tweed suit."

"If I begin to feel warm I'll tell you. Don't you want to walk?"

"Me? I'm the greatest walker in Paris. I told you that."

She took his arm. "Which way?"

They started down the street. There were other strollers, most of them ambling along leisurely, enjoying the walk for its own sake, no apparent destination in mind. Eddie could easily spot the tourists, even those who had left their cameras back in their hotel rooms.

"Henry James said something interesting about the thoughts you get while walking," said Eddie. "He called it the rich, ripe fruit of perambulation."

Connie looked startled.

"What's the matter?" asked Eddie. "I suppose you think the only James I should know is Harry."

She smiled and clutched his arm tighter.

Eddie remembered a remark a friend of his had once made about a girl: "I'm going to break up with her. She's not the type of girl you'd take for a walk on a Sunday afternoon."

He'd wondered at the time what type of girl it was you'd take for a walk on a Sunday afternoon. Now he knew.

And it felt good to see the way Connie reacted to the things she saw as they strolled along: the brightly colored awnings that covered café blending into café, the different types of people seated at the cafés, the fountains (even though they weren't running), the buildings, statues, the children sailing their boats in the ponds, even the tiny dandelion-like pollen that floated in the Paris air on this particular day.

He enjoyed her enjoyment of it all, her sense of wonder. Now she was beginning to get a feeling of the real Paris, his Paris. Now she would understand why he'd chosen to live here, why he could never be homesick for the States. Paris was something to be proud of, something to show off, as though it were his private possession.

"It's a wonderful city, isn't it?"

"It's beautiful, all right," she replied, "but, I don't know, don't you get the feeling once in a while that it's all sort of dead?"

He'd meant it as a rhetorical question. Dead? What did she mean by dead?

"Sort of passé? Don't misunderstand me. I find it all very interesting, and very lovely. But there's a sort of vitality lacking. I don't know, everything's so old. Nothing seems to be really *alive*."

She had seemed to be getting such a kick out of walking around that this was the last thing he'd expected her to say. What did she mean by *dead?* He knew. It was something he'd felt himself once in a while recently, the few times he permitted himself to think about it.

By his pride in the city he had been trying to fool himself as well as her. Look, a diamond! But she knew that it was only cut-glass sparkling in the sun, reflecting a frozen picture out-of-date and interesting-only-historically and for these reasons as grotesque as the gargoyles they saw when they finally reached Notre-Dame. For a while he'd been able to forget. Her reference to Paris as a dead city forced back the memories.

The Cathedral depressed him. He was glad when they left.

As they sat having coffee at a nearby café, Connie asked, "Do you want to call it quits now?"

"What?"

"I can go on by myself. You don't have to spend any more time with me. It seems to be such an effort for you. You seem to be so unhappy about it.".

Eddie was disturbed that Connie felt this way. "Not at all."

"Well something's the matter."

"Something happened this morning." He told her about Michel. That wasn't the only thing that was bothering him but at least it would allay Connie's fears that she was the cause of his restless discontent.

"I knew you were disturbed about something," said Connie. "But do they do that regularly—try to beat confessions out of people?"

"I don't know if they do it regularly," said Eddie. "But it's a known fact that they do it."

"Your free France," said Connie sarcastically.

"I suppose they don't do it back in America," he said. "Everyone knows about the American cops—the way they use the third degree."

"Why must you always refer back to America?" asked Connie. "Every time I criticize France you come back with a criticism of America. Can't you admit that France isn't perfect?"

"Okay!" he shouted.

She sat back in her chair. "I'm sorry. I didn't mean to upset you. Either way it doesn't help Michel."

"I don't know what would help Michel. I know his brother won't. Arrogant little pipsqueak. Ashamed that Michel's a jazz musician. Funny thing is if I hadn't met the brother I never would've suspected it. Michel always spoke about him in such glowing terms. He always looked up to him. For all I know maybe Michel himself was ashamed of playing jazz. I never thought of it. Maybe that's why he decided to teach, why he wanted all those letters of recommendation."

"Eddie . . . why don't we visit Michel now?"

He was thinking about what he had just said, wondering if it was really true. Michel ashamed because of his family. Family approval meant so much in France. And some of the French Negroes did look down upon the American Negroes, particularly the jazz musicians.

He recalled the time he was jostled in the street by two extremely well dressed African Negroes. They quickly apologized but he had the strange feeling that their bumping into him had been no accident.

"Eddie . . ."

"What? Visit Michel? A fine place to take a date—a hospital for mental disorders."

She leaned forward. "I wouldn't mind. And I know it would make you feel better if you could see him."

She was an understanding, considerate girl. He was angry at himself for having snapped at her. He thought of their first meeting at the Pam-Pam Bar and the way he had stomped off without even saying good-by. It was a wonder she had agreed to go out with him after that. It wasn't that she was intrigued because he had been nasty to her. That had happened to him before and he could easily spot that I-love-you-because-you-treat-me-cruel attitude some girls had. No, with Connie it was that she was understanding, that she saw beneath the surface explosion, that she saw something which he knew all along was there but was himself afraid to look at. She was a nice girl. She had more stature and substance than any girl he had known before.

He called to the waiter for the check. "I don't know if it'll do any good, our seeing him, but anyway you'll meet the greatest hot guitarist since Django Reinhardt."

She looked impressed, but he had a hunch that she had never heard of Django Reinhardt.

"You are very sweet, my dear," said Michel. He had a high-pitched voice that seemed to take the edge off his thick French accent. "But you must excuse my appearance. They took away my belt and my shoelaces."

There were several others in the visitors' room of the ancient Aisle de Charenton. The room was bare except for a few tables and chairs. The barred windows were set high up in the walls. Most of the patients sat quietly talking to their visitors, but one man paced nervously back and forth alongside a side wall, his head hung low, his hands behind him, mumbling to himself. His visitors they seemed to be his parents—did not even attempt to communicate with him.

Michel turned to Connie and said, "A fine place he brought you to meet me."

"It's all right, Michel," said Eddie. "You don't have to be ashamed. She's a good friend of mine."

"The way I look . . ." He brought his hand to his puffed-up face.

They must have given him quite a working over, thought Eddie. The left half of his face in particular was badly swollen.

"What they did to me . . ."

And what you've done to yourself, thought Eddie. *Why?*

"I'm sure you'll feel better in a few days," said Connie.

"She's very sweet," said Michel. "But why did you bring her to meet me here? I didn't expect you to come here, Eddie. They said they were going to get in touch with my brother. I'm surprised he hasn't come yet. He will be terribly angry with me. The disgrace of it all . . . I shouldn't have been sent here . . . a crazy house . . . I don't know why they wouldn't believe me . . . I recognized that woman as a friend of Stravinsky's. I'm sure he gave her a letter for me. But she's always had it in for me. She didn't want to give it to me. Why do so many of my friends have it in for me, Eddie?"

"Nobody has it in for you, Michel."

"Wait until I get out of here. I'm going to give it to my landlady. I know she's been holding back some of the letters. She's probably been opening them to find if there's any money in them."

"Your brother will probably be here tomorrow," said Eddie. "Is there anything we can do for you meanwhile?"

"Perhaps bring you some fruit or candy?" suggested Connie.

"You might stop by my place and see if I have any mail. Don't send it to me here. They'd probably take it away from me. Just hold onto it for me until I get out. Guard it carefully, for it may be valuable."

A white-jacketed attendant entered and announced that all patients had to return to their rooms.

"What's wrong with him, Doctor?" Eddie sat in the small, neatly furnished office of Dr. Kaval, one of the staff psychiatrists.

"It's complicated," answered the doctor. "I can't give you a simple diagnosis like paranoia or schizophrenia. It will take a few days of observation to find out. We do know that he's been sick a long time."

"What can I do to help?"

"There's nothing you can do. Not now."

Dr. Kaval was cooperative and unhurried but Eddie didn't want to keep Connie waiting outside in the ante room. He stood up.

"May I call you in a few days to find out how he is?"

"Certainly."

"Do you think he can be cured?"

"First let us try to determine what's the matter with him."

"Thank you for seeing me."

"Not at all."

They shook hands and Eddie left.

"What now?" asked Connie. They stood outside the gates of the hospital.

"I don't know. I feel bad about Michel."

"Was he a good friend of yours?"

"Not really. I don't think he was a good friend of anyone's. He played it pretty much solo. Kind of a queer duck."

"Just the same I can understand how upset you must be. I don't know him at all and it's depressed me terribly."

"Not a very enjoyable Paris-by-Day tour."

"Don't be silly. What else did I have to do today?"

"I'm sure you could have thought of something better than visiting a mental hospital."

"I didn't mind. Besides, the day isn't over."

"That's right. What else would you like to do? Anything special you'd like to see? Any place you'd like to go?"

"You're the guide!"

"I thought we'd stay clear of the tourist places—the Eiffel Tower, the Arc de Triomphe, Versailles. I thought . . . you know, how about doing what a Frenchman and his girl might do on an afternoon like this?"

"Anything you say. . . ."

"The Bois de Boulogne and a boat ride on the lake."

"You're sure you don't mind rowing?" he asked.

"I like it."

"I must be getting old. I didn't think I'd get tired that fast."

"I guess you don't do this too often."

"As a matter of fact this is the first time I've ever taken a boat out here. I've walked in this park many times. But this is the first time I've actually taken a boat out. Be sure to let me know when you're tired."

"I'm fine for now."

The lake was crowded with rowers, mostly young couples and families with small children.

"I love the way the French children look," Connie said. "They look like children."

"What do you mean?"

"Well I guess it's partly the way they're dressed. Back in America we've taken to dressing our kids like adults. From diapers to long pants. Or so it seems to me. They look like midgets. They certainly don't look like children."

"That's strange," said Eddie. He closed his eyes and tilted his face toward the sun. "In America the accent is supposed to be on youth.

Only the other day Benny said he's too old to go back to America. He's forty-five."

Eddie wondered how old Connie was. Twenty-eight or twenty-nine at the most. He wondered whether Marie had hit fifty yet. Michel was probably the youngest of the lot of them. Poor Michel.

"It's funny," he said, still keeping his eyes closed and his head tilted back, "the doctor couldn't say what was wrong with him. He said it would take a few days to find out."

"Michel?"

"Yes."

"The trouble is we know so little about the human mind," said Connie. "Psychiatry today is about where chemistry was in the days of the alchemists."

"Here in France they call mental illness the American's disease. There's so little of it here. Michel is the first Frenchman I know who's had a nervous breakdown."

Connie stopped rowing and allowed the boat to drift by itself. "What do you think brought it on?"

"Maybe it's contagious," said Eddie. "Maybe he's been hanging around too many Americans."

"You're bitter."

"Maybe I've a right to be."

"Maybe."

"Watch out for the boat," he warned.

Connie turned around, saw another boat headed toward them. There was plenty of time to get out of its way. A few quick strokes and they were clear of it.

"Maybe I've a right to be bitter, too," she said. "But I'm not."

"Good for you."

"You needn't be so sarcastic. Do you really hate America that much?"

"I think it stinks."

"If you were living in Paris because you liked it better here than back home I could understand that. But to have such hatred . . . I sometimes get the feeling that you're protesting too much. Don't you think you'll ever go back?"

"A friend of mine went back last year. Another musician. The first night off the boat he went into one of those big drugstores on Broadway where they sell everything. He said he looked around at the people rushing in and out, at their sad, beaten faces, at the garish displays, at all the junk they were selling and he let out one long scream and two days later he was back in Paris."

"But do you really feel at home here?"

"More at home than I've ever felt anywhere else. More at home than I ever did in Kansas City or New York."

She started rowing again, long, slow strokes. "It's amazing."

"It's not only the fact that I'm a Negro. In America everything's business, rushing around, commercialism. They're not only against Negroes. They're against themselves. They don't know how to live. They're their own worst enemies. I've no desire to go back."

"That wasn't the impression I got when we first met," said Connie. "I got the feeling you wanted to go back."

"Wrong impression."

"I still get that feeling."

"You're wrong."

"Be honest."

"Well . . . maybe sometimes I do think about going back. No matter how lousy your home was, there are always times when you think of going back to it . . . at least for a visit. But luckily every time

I get to feeling that way I bump into some American tourists and I realize how stupid the idea is."

"Thanks!"

"You know I don't mean you." He dipped his hand into the lake and playfully flicked a few drops of water at her.

"Hey!" she pleaded, laughing.

He smiled.

"That's the first time I've seen you smile all day."

"I guess I'm not the smiling kind," said Eddie.

"No. You're more the brooding, Hamlet type."

"Not really," said Eddie. "It's just that . . . I don't know why I keep thinking about Michel."

A boat skimmed by closely, almost colliding with them. In it were a young French couple, sitting side by side, paying more attention to each other than to rowing.

Few American tourists came to the Bois, except during the racing season when they visited the track. Eddie was glad he had taken Connie here. And yet he also felt sad. All around him were young French couples; some were kissing out in the open, with great passion, oblivious to everything around them; others just looked at one another, and it was obvious that they were in love—if only for the afternoon.

They rowed in silence a while. To keep the boat from turning in circles Eddie took his oar out of the water every now and then while Connie rowed.

"We're doing better with the two of us rowing," said Connie.

"But where are we going?"

"Let's go to the end of the lake, then back," said Connie.

"Okay."

The boat picked up speed until Eddie said, "Hey, let's take it easy. There's no rush."

They rowed more slowly.

"Eddie, are you really happy here?"

"Do you mean right here with you?"

"I didn't mean that. I meant here in Europe. Do you really feel accepted?"

Immediately he recalled his first concerts in France after the war— how he felt the French people had cheered and applauded him because he was a Negro. It hadn't been real acceptance. It had been sort of reverse-discrimination. Some of the other Negroes, of course, loved this attitude, played it for all it was worth. It had embarrassed and annoyed him. But all that was in the past, at the beginning of his stay in Paris. It was different now. Now he was accepted.

"Why is it so hard for you to believe that I could be accepted here?" asked Eddie.

"It's just that you still seem so American to me. Do the French *really* like jazz?"

"Try to get tickets to hear Wild Man Moore."

"But he's such a clown."

"Next to Louis Armstrong he's the best trumpeter around."

"Don't you think they might go to see him cut up rather than to hear him play?"

"And me? What about me?" he asked bitterly. "Why do you think they come to hear me play?"

"With you it's different. You don't carry on the way he does. I'm sure they like the way you play."

"Thanks."

"But I'm sure the Americans would like it even more. I don't know if the French can really appreciate jazz. It's basically foreign to them."

"We play pure jazz. And in art the French are purists. They know the real McCoy."

"I wonder."

She had stopped rowing.

"Getting tired?" He put his arm around her to reach the other oar.

"Do you want me to move to the back of the boat?" she asked.

"No, stay here." He was getting annoyed with her, but he liked having his arm around her, feeling her body close up against his, feeling their thighs touching.

"What makes you so sure the French don't really appreciate jazz?" he asked.

"I'm not sure. It's just a general impression."

"Based on one night at Marie's Cave?"

"I don't see how they could understand it."

"They do. Take it from me they do. I've been playing it to them for twelve years."

She shrugged her shoulders.

He was close to her he had his arm around her and yet he knew they were not together. They had stopped rowing and they sat in silence as they just drifted.

#《12》

BENNY WAS getting impatient waiting for Lillian in her hotel room. He had stretched himself out on her bed, his hands behind his head.

Although he had been up all night he wasn't tired. Not yet. Well, maybe a little tired but certainly not as exhausted as he knew he would be later on in the afternoon. This was the usual pattern. It wasn't the first time he had gone through the night without any sleep. Usually the effect of such a night didn't hit him until about three o'clock in the afternoon, and then when it finally did hit him he became so tired that he could easily fall asleep on his feet no matter where he was.

Generally it had been only on the nights of the jam sessions that he went without sleep. During the past year or two, however, there had been other nights as well, nights when he was too troubled to sleep.

He looked at his watch. He had been waiting for Lillian for over an hour.

Most often the things that troubled him didn't mean anything in themselves. They were little things he had done during the day, or perhaps something he knew he shouldn't have said, or something someone had said to him. Unimportant things, but he couldn't help worrying about them. What was worse, he couldn't help worrying that he was worrying.

His attitude toward Michel bothered him. The poor guy was a nut. He shouldn't have thrown him out of his apartment that time. And why did he resent him so? His feelings should be of pity, not anger or resentment. From now on he'd treat him differently—try to be more friendly toward him.

He rolled onto his side and stared at the closed door. He hoped Lillian would return soon.

One thing about Eddie . . . he always played it cool. Of course, he had problems like everyone else. There was the time Eddie and Marie broke up. Losing someone like Marie would've driven a lot of guys right off their rockers. Eddie just kept going. He continued working for her and they continued being good friends. It was funny how the world could cave in on some people and they'd keep going as though nothing had happened, while other people would be knocked off their pins by the littlest things. Eddie played it cool.

There was the other night at the club. "Nigger, I said play *Melancholy Baby!*" Jesus, if someone had called him a kike or a sheeny he'd smash his face in. Yet this slob called Eddie a nigger and all he did was to stop playing and look up and stare at him with hardly any expression on his face.

It was terrible. He himself had felt like killing the dirty bastard. He was glad that the French gal in the place had given it to him and Marie had kicked him and his party out. Of course, he didn't like the way some of the French people cursed them out for being Americans. He never liked that.

He rolled onto his back and stared up at the ceiling. It was funny how he had overcome his own prejudice toward Negroes. In fact, it wasn't until he stopped thinking of guys as Negroes or whites that he realized he had been prejudiced. As a kid in his neighborhood in Brooklyn, there were only two types of Negroes with whom he ever came into contact: cleaning girls and whores. Before the depression all of the families in the neighborhood had colored girls who came in to clean two or three times a week. He accepted without thinking about it the yiddish word for them: *shvartses*. And all the time he was a kid he thought of all Negroes as *shvartses*.

Then when he and his friends were fifteen or sixteen and couldn't wait to do what they had been talking about for the past eight or nine years, they found out from some new kids in the neighborhood that colored whores could be picked up on Lenox Avenue around 110th Street for a dollar. For two dollars a really nice one could be had and around the corner in a big apartment house on 100th Street facing the park there was a whorehouse where for five dollars you could have light skinned beauties who would do anything you wanted them to. He and his friends didn't have the five dollars for the house but they did have enough for the streetwalkers, and one Saturday afternoon four of them went down and they all did it to one girl. She charged five dollars for the four of them. After that they started going to Harlem regularly, and once he and a pal splurged and visited the house. And that's all he knew about Negroes: *shvartses* or whores. He didn't dislike them for it. He just didn't know there were any other kind.

Until he discovered jazz. And then there were three kinds: *shvartses*, whores and jazz musicians. Until he became friendly with some of the jazz musicians and got to know their friends and families, and got to know Harlem. Then he knew better. Getting into jazz music, getting with the boys who played it, had given him a new outlook on Negroes. A new outlook on a lot of things.

On girls, for instance. Among the Jewish families of Brooklyn there were only two kinds of girls, the good ones or the bad ones, the kind you screwed or the kind you married, the virgins or the whores, and they were whores even if they didn't do it for money, just as long as they did it. But once he started touring with the bands, once he met the girlfriends the guys had in the different cities they played on the road, once he started getting fixed up with some of them himself, he saw that a girl didn't have to be a whore to do it, that she could put out just because she liked a guy, even though she knew there was no chance of anything permanent coming from it, even though she knew that the chances were she'd never see the guy after that night. And it was okay. They were good kids. And all that crap that his mother and father had drummed into him about good girls and bad girls was just that—a lot of crap.

Much as he had hated the road, he had to admit it had been a great education. For a while, anyway. Then it became a drag. The one-night stands with the college kids, playing the same rigidly orchestrated music over and over and over again, the all-day bus rides, the cheap hotels, the lousy restaurant food, the poker games, whisky, the thick cloud of cigarette smoke, or marihuana smoke. And then later, for some of the guys, the stronger stuff, first sniffing it and then taking it in the arm with the needle. He himself had never tried *H*—he never would in a million years—but he could understand how some of them who had been doing the road bit for a long time would be driven to it. Anything to escape. God, how he'd hated touring with the bands.

Sure he'd been making good money, especially for those depression years when so many of his friends and relatives were out of work, including his own father, but he'd hated it just the same. And he knew his parents hated it, too. This wasn't what they imagined he'd be doing when his father used to put aside five hard-earned bucks each week for his piano lessons. He stuck with the long-hair stuff a while—he liked it well enough—but he liked jazz better. And then when the depression came along it was a question of making money any way you could. And so he started to play jazz. Except it really wasn't jazz. Not the kind he wanted to play. It was the era of the touring name bands—swing. After the novelty of traveling had worn off, it became painful, torturous.

More and more he was drawn back to Dixieland. Late at night when the crowd had gone and a single worklight burned on the stand he and some of the boys in the band would spend the hours before dawn jamming away Dixieland. It was their outlet, their safety-valve. Without those sessions he didn't know how he would have been able to bear the swing music they had to play every night.

One January he received a telephone call from his father telling him that he should come home right away because his mother was very ill with pneumonia. He could tell from the way his father sounded that she was already dead. He came home for the funeral and then rejoined the band back on the road. A few months later he got another telephone call. His father had killed himself by jumping off the roof of their six-story tenement. Once again he returned home. Only this time, after the week of mourning that followed the funeral, he didn't return to the band. He moved in with his aunt and for the next few years did nothing—moped around the house, hung out around the candy store with all the other guys out of work, took in a lot of movies. Once in a while he'd play some Dixieland, just for the fun of it, with some of the musicians he'd bump into downtown. Two days after Pearl Harbor was bombed he enlisted in the army.

He was put into the infantry, which naturally enough he hated violently, and when a notice appeared on the barracks bulletin board asking musicians who wanted to get into Special Services to appear in the Orderly Room the next morning he was the first one on line.

It was shortly after the war had ended that he met Eddie in Paris. They both were still in the army and Eddie told him about his plan to get discharged in Europe and organize a small combo to tour army installations for the War Department. It sounded like a great idea to Benny and after Eddie heard Benny tickle the ivories he was only too happy to make him part of his band.

All those tours, all those years together. Over ten years ago, and it seemed like yesterday. Life was shooting by too fast, too fast.

"You!"

The piercing cry interrupted his reverie. It was Lillian. He hadn't heard her open the door. She had a startled expression on her face. She held her hand up in front of her, as though in self-defense. "What are you doing here?"

As Benny swung around to a sitting position on the edge of the bed the heel of his shoe left a streak on the bedspread.

"On my bed," moaned Lillian. "And with your shoes on! Look what you did!"

"I'm sorry. I'm terribly sorry." He stood up and brushed the dirt off with his hand. "C'mon in, don't just stand there."

She entered the room, slowly, hesitatingly. She clutched her pocketbook to her breast. They stared at each other without saying anything. Slowly she brought the pocket book down to her side. Slowly she relaxed.

"I'm sorry about last night," said Benny. "That's why I'm here. I came to apologize."

"How did you get in?"

"I came with Eddie. Connie was here. They left and I stayed. I felt a little tired so I stretched out on the bed."

"With your shoes on!"

He brushed the bedspread with his hand again, though there was no longer any dirt showing.

"It seems to be all right now," she said.

He brushed it once or twice more for good measure. He nervously ran his hand up and down the side of his trousers. "That was quite a night we had last night."

"It was terrible."

"I don't know what got into me," said Benny. "I didn't go to bed at all; I just sat up and worried about it."

Lillian looked puzzled. Benny scratched his head.

"Lately I do all sorts of silly things and then I'm sorry afterward. I don't know why I do them in the first place. I didn't mean to take you to those places last night. I'm sorry I did."

"It wasn't that bad," said Lillian.

Benny, who had been staring at the floor, looked up at her, hopefully.

"Of course I didn't enjoy any of it," said Lillian. "Far from it! Especially the pool."

"I could kill myself."

"Then why did you do it?"

"I don't know!"

"I should have been more firm in refusing to go." She sank into a chair. "But I drank so much I guess I didn't know what I was doing."

"It was all my fault," said Benny. "The way I kept pouring the stuff into you."

"Don't remind me of it," said Lillian. She rubbed her brow.

"Hangover?"

"Splitting headache!"

Benny nodded his head. "Hangover!"

"I thought the air might make me feel better. It didn't."

"Did you eat anything?"

"I had to force it down." She crossed to the closet and started to take out her valise. Benny jumped to her assistance. "Could you put it on the bed?" she asked.

When she opened the valise he saw that it was full of her things. "You haven't unpacked?"

"I feel safer with the clothes in my valise. Those dresser drawers don't seem very clean." She rummaged through her things and finally located a small leather box. It was stamped with gold lettering: *Medi-Kit.* She opened it. Inside were half a dozen labeled vials with different colored pills. She took two tablets out of the one marked Anacin. "I seem to react peculiarly to aspirin," she explained. "I hope these Anacin tablets do the trick."

She poured some water into a paper cup from a half filled bottle of Perrier atop the dresser and swallowed the tablets.

Benny felt terribly sorry for her. "What are you going to do today?"

"We've no planned activities for the day," replied Lillian. "I suppose I should rest and try to get rid of this headache."

"How about going for a ride in the country? I know where I could borrow a car."

She put the pillbox back in the valise and Benny put the valise back in the closet.

"Well, how about it?"

"No thank you," she replied, but Benny knew that she was interested. All it would take was a little coaxing.

"Aw, come on. . . ."

"I ought to stay close to the hotel."

"Don't hold last night against me. I told you I was sorry. I promise, nothing like that today."

"I don't feel too well, I—"

"It's just a hangover; it's nothing serious. Hanging around the hotel room moping and feeling sorry for your self won't help any. If you get out you'll forget about yourself and feel better."

"Where'll we go?"

"There are some lovely places right outside the city. The country air and sunshine will be good for you."

She sat on the edge of the chair trying to decide.

"I won't do anything to shock you this time. I promise."

"I wouldn't want to go too far away—in case I suddenly felt worse."

"We could go to the park, then. The Luxembourg Gardens or the Bois. We could have some lunch and then later, if you felt better, we could go for a ride."

She hesitated.

"Be a sport," he pleaded. "Let me make up for what happened last night."

"Well," she said, "Maybe it would be nice to go to the park for a little while."

As they walked to the bus stop Lillian drew Benny's attention to a small cylindrical metal structure that stood on the corner of the street. As one man walked out of it another man entered.

"I've noticed those things before," said Lillian. "What are they?"

"Pissoirs."

"What?"

"Pissoirs. In case you have to take a lea—I mean, well, a Frenchman drinks a lot of wine, you know, and what goes in has to come out and, well, they're very convenient."

She looked at him with a half-angry expression on her face. "And a moment ago you promised that you weren't going to shock me anymore!"

For a second he thought she was serious. "It—it's not my fault," he stammered, "that's what they happen to be, I'm not . . ." But then he saw her smile and they both laughed as they continued on toward the bus stop.

As they entered the Luxembourg Gardens Lillian stopped in surprise before a young man sitting alone on a bench. "Martin Weiner, what are you doing here?"

"Oh, hi," said Martin. "Just taking in the sights."

Lillian introduced him to Benny and the three of them sat down together.

"What a pleasure it is to have a day off from culture," said Martin. "This sure is a pretty park."

The elm trees, the arches of ivy, the meticulously trimmed hedges, the carefully tended flower beds were all in full bloom. Groups of children stood around the huge octagonal basin watching their fleet of small boats. On nearby benches several couples necked unashamedly.

"That's what I like about the French," said Martin, "they're so uninhibited. That's if they know you. Try to pick one up, though, that is if she's a respectable girl. Brother!"

"Martin, I'm surprised at you," said Lillian.

"Only to talk to I mean," explained Martin. "To find out what they're like."

"There are several nice young girls in our group. You should be more friendly with them."

"What for?" asked Martin. "I didn't come to Europe to get friendly with Americans. I came to get friendly with the Europeans."

"He's right," said Benny. There are plenty of Americans back in America. What does he need them here for? Stick around, kid, I'll introduce you to some nice French girls."

Martin's face lit up.

"Are you kidding?"

"No, I mean it."

"Benny, please," protested Lillian. "Don't you think Martin is a little young for the kind of girls you know?"

Martin's face lit up even more. He looked quizzically at Lillian, as though to ask what she was doing with a fellow like Benny.

"What are you talking about," said Benny. "I know some very nice girls. And I'll be glad to arrange for you to meet some of them."

"We're leaving in a few days," said Martin, anxiously.

"I'll make a few calls later," said Benny. "You're staying at Lillian's hotel?"

"That's right."

Benny nodded his head. "I'll take care of it." He could see that Lillian didn't approve. "Believe me," he said to her, "they're very nice girls. One of them is even a schoolteacher."

"Next time I come to Europe I'm going to come alone," said Martin. He looked at Lillian. "Not that the people in our group aren't nice," he added, "but I think that for a fellow it's more fun if he goes alone. I really wanted to go alone this time but my mother and father said they wouldn't let me go unless I went on a tour." He turned to Benny. "You're not on a tour, are you?"

Benny quickly explained what he did and how long he had been living in Paris. This seemed to compound Martin's surprise that Lillian should be with Benny.

"Gee, it must be great to live in Paris all the time," he said, "especially without having to go to a different museum every day." He looked at the couples necking. "I'd love to be able to live here all the time."

"Don't be silly," said Benny. "Sure, enjoy it all you can while you're here. But don't forget how lucky you are to be able to go home."

"What do you mean by *able* to go home?" Martin asked. "Aren't you *able* to go home?"

"Oh yeah," said Benny, "sure I'm able to go home, any time I want to. I meant don't be sorry that after the trip is over you'll be going home, that's all. I could go home, too, but this is where I make my living."

"But surely," interrupted Lillian, "you could make a living doing what you're doing back in America?"

"I don't know," said Benny. "I hear things are pretty tough for musicians back there now." He was anxious to change the topic. "Anyway, kid, don't worry about meeting those French girls. I'll fix you up. I'll arrange something and call you later at the hotel."

"Thanks a lot," said Martin, "I'll be looking forward to it." He stood up. "Well, I think I'm going to continue wandering around. See you later at dinner, Lillian. Nice to have met you, Mr. . . ."

"Benny. Keep it informal," said Benny.

"Okay, Benny." They shook hands and Martin walked off.

"Nice kid," said Benny.

"Very nice," said Lillian. "I don't think he's too happy, though. One man among nineteen women and most of them older than he."

"I can imagine," said Benny, "although I don't think I'd particularly mind a set-up like that."

Lillian took a handkerchief out of her purse and wiped her forehead.

"How do you feel?" asked Benny.

"Oh, much better now, thank you. A little warm, but I think the headache's going away." She looked around. "This is much pleasanter than last night."

"There's a beautiful fountain down a ways," said Benny. "The Medicis fountain. Would you like to see it?"

"Let's rest here a moment, if you don't mind."

"Anything you say."

From the way she looked at him Benny knew that she was no longer angry over what had happened last night.

She was all right, Benny thought. She was a good sport. The chances were the kids who had her for a teacher liked her. And then suddenly he understood why he had tried to embarrass her the night before: it was because she was a teacher. She had reminded him of the countless college and university dances he had played for back in the States during the depression and the word "Wasp" flashed across his mind. How he used to hate the laughter and joyous cavorting on the dance floor of the Wasps.

"Wasp" was the word a fellow Jewish musician had taught him. It stood for White Anglo-Saxon Protestant, the *American* American, the only one who didn't have to worry about filling in the blanks after Race and Religion on the job applications. The Wasps didn't know from the depression. They waited it out dancing at the frat house or cheering themselves hoarse in the football stadium after Jack Oakie and Lew Ayres made that last quarter touchdown that saved the game for dear Alma Mater. And always present, always watching over their young Wasp charges, were the older Wasp chaperons, the House Mother or House Father or Dean of Women's Activities. *And so often they looked like Lillian.*

It was a life denied him, a life he hated, and yet a life he helped make pleasanter by providing it with a musical background. How often, as he sat on his weary butt playing *Dancing in the Dark*, watching the young crew-cut male Wasps cheek to cheek with their pretty blond bobbed-hair female Wasps, overlooked by the older Lillian-like Wasp chaperons, he had wished he could throw a bomb in their midst even if it meant that he himself would be destroyed by it. He wanted to get back at these Wasps who could sting so painfully with only a look.

Lillian had stood for the Wasps. Only she was out of her territory now. She was in his territory. It had made her vulnerable. He looked at Lillian. She was a Wasp. Yet here in Paris, sitting in the Luxembourg Gardens, there was no sting in her look.

She smiled at him. There was only kindness and forgiveness and understanding and maybe a little self-pity and regret. Certainly there was no sting.

"Let me know when you're rested," he said. "I'll show you the fountain. I don't know if the water's running, but it'll be interesting to see anyway."

《 13 》

"It's a nice place," said Connie.

"It'll do."

"I like the way you've decorated it."

"It's all right."

"What's the view like?" She pulled up the blinds that covered the glass doors and stepped out on the balcony. "Very nice."

She stepped back into the room. Eddie started to pull the blinds down again.

"Leave them up," she said.

He let go of the cord. There was still the tension between them that had sprung up during their tiff in the rowboat. He was surprised that she had accepted his invitation to come up to his apartment.

"The bedroom is small," he said. "And there's not much of a kitchen."

She walked to the bedroom door. "May I?"

"Sure."

She opened it and looked inside. "This isn't bad at all. And you keep it very neat. You should see the size of my place in Chicago." She crossed the room and entered the kitchen.

"It's a darling little kitchen. Do you do much cooking here?"

"Hardly any at all."

"Refrigerator, too. All the comforts of home."

"Can I fix you a drink?" he asked.

"Not right now, thank you."

"I'm going to make myself one." He poured himself a cognac. "Would you like some coffee?"

"Nothing, now."

They returned to the living room.

Eddie sipped his drink. "So jazz bores you," he said.

"I see I have to be careful about what I say to you. You never forget a thing."

"Not anything as important as that. Jazz is more than the way I make my living."

"I really didn't mean it," she said. "I guess it's because I was sore at you—always attacking America, always defending the French."

Eddie put his drink down. "You spoke before about protesting too much. You remind me of Benny. I think both of you protest too much every time America is criticized. Why are both of you so sensitive about it? Is it because you know there's too much truth in what's said? Is it because both of you really hate America as much as I do but you haven't the guts to face up to it?"

Eddie noticed her uneasiness.

"I keep telling you I don't hate America," she said. "I keep telling you I like America; I think it's probably the best country in the world, even with its faults. But you don't seem to believe me. I don't know what I can do to prove to you that I mean it."

"If what you say is true you must be awfully thick skinned about being a Negro," he said. "Either that or you've been awfully lucky."

He saw her hand tighten on the edge of the chair. He knew that he was goading her on, building up rage within her. But this was what he wanted to do. He felt the need of encouraging an explosion between them.

"How dare you say such a thing to me!" she snapped at him. "Because I don't whine or complain all the time you think I'm thick-skinned? Because I don't bemoan the life I've led or try to run away from it by becoming a bitter expatriate you think I've been lucky?"

This reference to *his* running away, *his* bitterness, hurt, but it was a pain not unmixed with pleasure. It was almost something he wanted to hear.

" Do you think it was easy for me to become a teacher?" she asked. "I mean a teacher in a white school? Do you know how many times I had to make believe I didn't hear certain things, didn't see certain things, didn't feel certain things?"

"And did you shuffle when you walked?"

She looked at him wide-eyed. She ran her tongue over her lower lip. "I always tried to walk with my head held high. I didn't always succeed but at least I tried. At least I didn't run away like a whipped dog with my ass dragging."

Her saying the word "ass" startled and titillated him. It was like an open sesame to a locked door. She hadn't always been the schoolteacher with the soft-spoken, carefully chosen words. What she knew didn't all come from books.

"I guess that's enough of that," he said.

She spoke calmly. "No, it's not enough. You start something and every time I try to defend myself you shut me up. It isn't very polite."

"I'm afraid I'm not a very polite guy."

"I'm afraid you're not a very healthy guy."

"More psychoanalysis, huh?"

"You invite me here, and then suddenly, for no reason at all, you try to pick a fight with me."

"You started it," said Eddie. "Back in the boat."

"I'm only human. You were beginning to get on my nerves."

"And maybe you're beginning to get on my nerves now," said Eddie.

She stood up. "I stopped fighting you back in the boat," she said. "But you don't want to stop fighting me now."

"Do you want a drink?"

"I'm leaving. That's what you want me to do, isn't it?"

He gulped down his drink. "Do what you want to do. If you want to leave, go."

Her hands trembled as she put on her gloves. He realized that he had embarrassed and upset her more than he had intended. He felt remorseful about it but he knew that he would get over this feeling, just as he had always got over it with all the other girls. He expected her to storm out, slamming the door behind her, but instead, after she had put on her gloves she sat down again and stared straight at him. He avoided her eyes.

"I can't figure you out," she said. "We had such a wonderful evening last night. You were so nice to me all day today. I admired you so much for the way you were concerned about your friend Michel. I thought we couldn't have hit it off better, even with our little political arguments. You're a Jekyll and Hyde. Suddenly you decide to end it all and you become angry and nasty and, yes, even hateful toward me. It's not only what you say but how you say it. You're like a completely different person."

She paused as though she expected him to say something. He remained silent.

"I feel terribly sorry for you," she went on. "I meant what I said before about your being unhappy. You must be terribly unhappy."

He looked at her and saw that she was now looking at him with a feeling of great pity. Why was she still sitting there? Why couldn't she just leave like all the others did?

"People who hate themselves," she continued, "are, I guess, the unhappiest people of all."

He saw that her anger and embarrassment had quickly subsided. She continued to look at him with pity in her eyes, searching, knowledgeable pity. More than looking at him, she was looking through him. It gave him a painfully uncomfortable feeling, because it cut deeply and honestly. He felt the perspiration on his face.

"Maybe you're right," he said.

She sat back in the chair. "I'll take that drink now," she said.

He went into the kitchen and brought her a cognac. His hand shook as he handed it to her.

"I'll go right after this," she said, sipping the drink.

"You don't have to."

"I guess I better."

"I'd rather you stayed."

"You certainly don't act that way."

"Please stay."

He was glad that she appeared uncertain.

"I'll take one of your English cigarettes," she said. "And perhaps a little more cognac."

He handed her a cigarette, lit it for her, brought the bottle of cognac in from the kitchen and filled their glasses.

She puffed on the cigarette.

Eddie knew that he more than liked Connie. He crossed over to her, sat on the arm of her chair, and kissed her. He kissed her again.

"This is silly," she said.

"I don't think so."

"Please let me get up."

"Why?"

"It'll be more comfortable on the couch."

He let her get up and cross to the couch. He turned down the blinds. They kissed several times and he moved his hand against her breast and down to her thighs.

"We'll be even more comfortable inside," he whispered, motioning with his head toward the bedroom.

She said nothing. He stood up and opened the bedroom door. Slowly she walked in and sat on the edge of the bed. He sat down next to her. He could see that she was excited, that she wanted him. And he wanted her. He put his arm around her and pulled her down alongside him. He turned on his side and drew her close. Suddenly, unexpectedly, she struggled to get free and bolted up.

"No, no, it's crazy," she said. "I can't, I just can't!"

He stood beside her and held her close. "There's nothing wrong with it."

"No, no, not this way. It's not right. I can't do it."

She pushed herself away from him and turned her back on him.

"Haven't you ever . . . before?"

"Yes, I've done it before," she said.

It was plain to him that she was terribly unnerved. He knew that the tactful thing to do would be to stop now, that even if she suddenly changed her mind it wouldn't be any good. But he wanted her very much.

"Then why not now?" he pleaded.

"Because it's different now."

She turned and faced him.

"I don't like one-night stands," she said. "I've had them before but only because I was curious. I'm a big girl now and I'm no longer curious. It has to mean something more now."

"I suppose I could tell you that I like you very much."

"And what could I tell you?" she asked.

She moved closer to him.

"I suppose I could tell you," she continued, "that now that I've proven to myself that I could be a teacher, that now that I've lived alone for four years, that now that I've made the trip to Europe I no longer want to be alone. I need someone now. I've really needed someone for a long time. But not someone that I'll give myself to for only one night because he says that he likes me very much."

"I think you must like me," he said. "At least I hope you do."

She went back to the living room and sat down on the couch. He followed her in and sat down on the chair opposite her.

"I'm sorry," he said.

"It's my fault," she replied. "I shouldn't have come here in the first place."

They sat without talking.

Eddie wondered what she was thinking about. "Would you ever consider living here in Paris?" he asked her.

"No. I could never do that."

"Why not?

"I don't belong here."

"If you gave yourself a chance?"

"No. I've seen your friends. They're bitter, they're dispossessed. They're people without roots."

"You mean that party last night? They're not all like that."

"It's not for me," she said. "I could never be happy here."

He stood up, crossed to the window, raised the blinds and looked out on the bustling late afternoon traffic on the boulevard below. Most of the traffic was going one way, people driving back after a weekend or a day in the country.

"Suppose I went back to the States . . ." He spoke slowly. "Could we continue seeing each other?"

"I don't see why not."

He stared down the boulevard he loved so well, at the trees and houses lining the boulevard. He reminded himself that he had never enjoyed any streets in any of the American cities as he did the streets of Paris.

"Would you come back to America?" Connie asked.

"I might," he said. "If—"

"If what?" She sounded as though she had been almost afraid to ask.

"If I loved you," he answered. "If I loved you I guess I might do anything."

"It's silly of us to talk this way," she said. "We hardly—"

"I know," he interrupted. "We hardly know each other."

"It's true, isn't it?"

"I don't know."

He took out his pack of English cigarettes. "Another cigarette?"

She shook her head no. He took one himself and lit it.

"How much longer are you going to stay in Paris?" he asked.

"We leave Friday for the Riviera."

"Will you be able to come to the club tomorrow night? It's our all-night jam session. Some of the top musicians in Paris sit in."

"Will Wild Man Moore be there?"

"Maybe."

He knew that he could invite her to the dinner which some of the boys were giving that evening for Wild Man Moore. But suddenly he felt he wanted a few hours away from her to think things over.

"One night this week," Connie said, "we're going to see the Comédie Française. I think it's Wednesday night. Thursday night we're going to see the Ballet in the court of the Louvre. All the other nights we're free. But of course you have to work at night."

"I'm free all during the day," said Eddie.

"Mrs. Vogel has planned something for each day," said Connie.

"Couldn't you get out of it?"

"I suppose so. I really better go now."

"I'll take you home."

"You've done enough taking me around for today," said Connie. "I'll manage by myself."

"I'd be glad to. . . ."

"I'd rather go home alone."

"May I call you early tomorrow morning?" he asked.

"Sure. But we leave for the Musée Nationale d'Art Moderne at ten sharp."

"I'll call you at nine."

"Won't that be early for you?"

"I'll call you at nine."

He held the door open for her. She put her arms around his neck and pressed herself close to him.

"We'll see each other tomorrow," she said.

She walked out of the apartment and started down the steps. He closed the door after her.

He stepped out onto the balcony. He saw her exit from the apartment house, take a few steps down the street and then turn around to look up at him. They smiled and waved to one another. He watched her as she continued walking down the street. At the end of the block she looked up at him once more and waved. Then she turned the corner and was out of sight.

He remained on the balcony, looking down the boulevard, feeling depressed.

❰❰ 14 ❱❱

ALMOST EVERYONE of any importance in the Paris jazz world was at the dinner at the Café Francis to honor Wild Man Moore. The only ones missing were some of the boys from Wild Man Moore's band and Wild Man Moore himself. They were expected to show any minute.

Eddie and Benny sat at the main table, together with the boys from Wild Man Moore's band: Hank Dixon, the trombone player; Skinny Sam, the piano man; and Oogie Edwards, the bass player. Bernie Shaw, the pianist who had gone "progressive," was also seated at the table. Bernie Shaw and Benny were the only white musicians there. The two other white musicians from Eddie's band, Len Smith and Mike Winters, were at one of the other tables.

The champagne and Scotch had been plentiful and Eddie knew that he'd been drinking too much of both.

The talk was loud, the stories tall, and while everybody was having a gay, lively time Eddie knew it would get much gayer and livelier once the elusive Wild Man Moore made his appearance.

"So I fixed the kid up with Carole, Suzie's younger sister," said Benny. "He went over there for dinner. He was so excited he couldn't thank me enough. I hope he isn't expecting too much. They're a very respectable family. Lillian didn't like the idea of my fixing him up at all. She is kind of prudish and a hick but a very sweet old lady underneath it all. I spent the whole day with her and now everything's squared away."

"That's nice," said Eddie morosely.

"This is getting to be like a seesaw," said Benny. "I'm low, you're high. I'm high, you're low. What's the matter, the girl give you a hard time today?"

"Hey, where's the boy?" shouted Len Smith.

137

"Yeah, where is he?" echoed Mike. "We're all starving here!"

"The hell with the food," said Len. "There won't be anything for him to drink by the time he gets here."

"Don't you get no gray hairs worryin' about his not showin'," said Hank Dixon.

"Maybe he stopped off to play a gig," said one of the other musicians.

"The three things Wild Man never fails to show for are friends, food and liquor," said Skinny Sam.

"You mean he's given up pussy?" asked still another musician. They all laughed.

"You know, Eddie," Benny said, "I never thought I'd take to chaperoning old ladies around Paris but, man, you should've seen me today. I was a regular Boy Scout."

"I'll get you a good-conduct medal," said Eddie.

"I enjoyed it. I tell you she's really a sweet old lady."

"You sound like you've fallen for her."

"Very funny," said Benny.

"You didn't take her back to the Piscine des Naturistes?"

"We went to the Luxembourg Gardens. Then I borrowed Len's car and we went for a ride in the country. When I took her back to the hotel I saw your girl. She looked kind of happy. Did you take good care of her? Not that I mean to get personal . . ."

Eddie looked at him askance.

"What are wrong?" asked Benny.

"You've got that idiotic look on your face," replied Eddie.

Benny dropped his smile.

One of the musicians at a nearby table stood up. He was obviously drunk. "I propose a toast," he said.

"Save it until Wild Man Moore shows," said Hank Dixon.

The two musicians sitting alongside the drunken one pulled him down to his seat.

Eddie wasn't enjoying himself. He felt the beginnings of a headache coming on. On his way over to the club he'd been looking forward to getting together with the boys from Wild Man Moore's band. It had been a long time since he had seen some of them. Now, however, sitting among them, looking them over one by one, seeing how they acted in each other's company, he realized how far removed he was from them. There was really nothing he had to say to any of them anymore.

He wished that instead of coming here he'd made a date with Connie. Why, when he felt he might be in love with her, did he want some time away from her? He wondered whether it was because he was afraid of being in love with her.

Len Smith pulled his chair over to the table and squeezed in next to Hank Dixon. "Man," he said, "I hear you cats caused quite a stir in Sweden."

"Oh, they dig us there," replied Hank. "We even had a few riots." He spoke loudly enough for all to hear him. "But man, those Swedish cats are making the big mistake. They're goin' for the new garbage, er, excuse me, I mean the new sounds. You know, the noise our good friend Bernie Shaw is dispensin'."

They all laughed. Eddie looked at Bernie and saw that he was taking it good-naturedly. He recalled Marie's boyfriend Varay suggesting that perhaps he should start playing like Bernie. He still couldn't figure out what Marie saw in Varay. As for Bernie Shaw he seemed like a nice enough fellow.

"It was in Copenhagen that they really dug us," continued Hank. "Man, that's where they dug us the most! In the middle of one concert at their big concert hall this big Denmark chick runs right up on the stage before anyone can stop her and gives Wild Man Moore a big kiss. You should've seen the expression on Wild Man's face! He was so busy blowin' he didn't even see her coming. The rest of us saw her and we stopped playin' as soon as we saw her jump on the stage. Wild Man, he don't know from nothin'! He's got his eyes closed and he's just blowin' away to beat the band. Next thing he knows this chick's got her arms around him. Suddenly he stops and almost drops his horn and she gives him a big kiss right on the mouth. We was laughin' so much we couldn't play.

"For five minutes we just stood there laughin' ourselves sick. The cats in the joint went crazy, screamin' and laughin' and clappin' their hands like mad. Then the chick goes back to her seat and sits down. Wild Man was fit to be tied. She was no crazy teenage chick like back home. She was a good-lookin' chick with fancy clothes, about forty. Wild Man's yellin' at us, 'You sonsofbitches why didn't you stop her!' and we're laughin' and laughin' and Wild Man's tellin' us to play and we're just standin' there laughin' and all the cats is goin' crazy cheerin' the chick who kissed him and finally old Skinny Sam here done break in playin' *Just a Kiss in the Dark* and we pick up on it, includin' Wild Man who's glad to see us stop laughin' and start to play, and them Copenhagen cats they start screamin' and cheerin' loudern ever until the cops come in an' try to quiet 'em down, but, man, after that there was no holdin' 'em down! What a ball!"

"That night," said Oogie Edwards, the bass player, "everybody scored! Man, them chicks wouldn't let us alone. If you don't jazz 'em they think you're insultin' 'em. And it's free! Give me Copenhagen any time!" He made an obscene motion with his arm and they all roared.

They really roared a second later when Wild Man Moore finally made his entrance. It was a screaming, thumping, jumping entrance, Wild Man Moore bounding in like a kangaroo, issuing his famous high-pitched cry. He leaped among the tables, greeting the boys by slapping them on the back or pushing their heads onto the table, or hugging and kissing them.

Entering after him, more reserved, his entourage: two young and beautiful French whores; Jess Bearden, his clarinetist; Iggy Walters, his drummer; and Mr. Seymour, his usually present white manager. Wild

Man Moore wore a free-flowing black bow tie and a tight-fitting red beret.

"Eddie, daddy, you son-of-a-bitch, give me some skin, you hear!" yelled Wild Man Moore, holding his open palm out. Eddie gave him some skin and Wild Man Moore howled, "That's a baby! That's a baby!" and playfully tapping the side of Eddie's chin, bounded over to another table and another musician he hadn't seen since his last trip to Europe.

Eddie suddenly felt glad to see Wild Man Moore.

"Oh shit," mumbled Benny to Eddie, "I didn't know that fink Seymour was coming along. I can't stand that vulture."

Neither could Eddie. He had met the short, skinny, nervous Mr. Seymour for the first time four years ago with Wild Man Moore and had seen him several times after that alone while Mr. Seymour was in Paris smelling around for new acts. He was a personal manager and booking agent and on the strength of having Wild Man Moore as a client was able to acquire and exploit lesser known acts. At least that was his reputation. The gag was that Mr. Seymour never discriminated. He'd take your money no matter what the color of your skin. He was aggressive in his manner of speaking and at the same time edgy and shifty-eyed, as though afraid of being caught.

Wild Man Moore, having finished personally greeting all of the boys, now stood in the center of the floor, his feet spread wide apart and his big hands held high in the air, and screeched his famous high-pitched cry. All the musicians returned it. The French waiters thought that they had all gone crazy. Then Wild Man Moore walked around the tables once again, holding the palms of his hands out so they could all give him some skin a second time.

Mr. Seymour, almost scowling, jerked his head in recognition of the boys in the restaurant and they all sat down.

"What's *he* doin' here?" asked Wild Man, pointing to Bernie Shaw. "I thought for sure he'd be dead by now. Playin' that Be-Bop is enough to kill any man!"

They laughed.

"There's only one thing Wild Man hates more than Be-Bop," said Jess, the clarinetist. "That's—now watch him have a fit—Rock 'n Roll!" He shouted the words "Rock 'n Roll" into Wild Man's face and Wild Man immediately reacted by banging his head on the table and issuing his cry. The musicians laughed hysterically.

No, Eddie realized, Wild Man Moore hadn't changed. He was as big a clown as ever.

"That is positively the worst!" screamed Wild Man. "That noise drove me right back to Europe!"

"But it sure seems to be the rage over there now," said Benny. "Mr. Seymour, is this something you're promoting?"

Mr. Seymour shook his head no.

"It's a sickness," said Wild Man Moore, "a real sickness! One of the boys told me just before we left about playin' his first and last Rock 'n Roll gig. Just before they went on he started to tune up and they said to him, 'Man, are you out of your mind? What the hell you tunin' up for? What do you think you are, a musician? We don't need no musicians here. We're playin' Rock 'n Roll!'"

"There's only one good thing about Rock 'n Roll," said Skinny Sam. "You can't play Rock 'n Roll and be a junkie, 'cause the noise blows the lid right off of your head!"

"Mr. Seymour," said Benny, "when are you going to make Wild Man play Rock 'n Roll? I understand that's what can really make a buck back in the States—Rock 'n Roll music."

"I like it about as much as Wild Man," said Mr. Seymour.

"Come off it," said Benny. "You know if Wild Man wanted to play it you'd be only too happy to let him, especially if a quick buck could be made from it."

"Still the wise guy, huh?" said Mr. Seymour. "When you gonna smarten up, boy?"

"Oh, I'm smart enough about certain things," replied Benny. "And I'm smart enough about certain people, too."

Eddie kicked Benny's leg under the table. He felt that this was neither the time nor the place for Benny to start up with Mr. Seymour. They all knew that Mr. Seymour owned and used Wild Man Moore like a crooked prize fight manager uses a naive pug, and they took this opportunity of Benny's crack to laugh much too hard for Mr. Seymour's comfort.

"Aren't you going to introduce us to the chicks?" asked Skinny Sam.

"Pardon me," said Wild Man. "Boys, meet my cousins!" They all laughed. The girls obviously didn't understand any English, but they wanted to be cooperative and laughed along with the crowd.

The waiters brought on the food and the musicians dug in like lumberjacks.

"Man," said Hank Dixon, "these frogs really know how to cook. I sure am going to be sorry when we shove out of here."

"How long you staying in Europe this trip?" asked Bernie Shaw.

"Four months this trip," Hank said. "And, man, I love every minute of it. When we tour back in the States it's a drag. One town looks like every other town. But over here each city's different. And after we get through playin', that's when the ball really begins!"

"We've really been livin' high off the hog," said Iggy, the drummer.

"I can't wait to get back to Munich," said Hank Dixon. "Man, that's the greatest. They got the clubs over there. In one club they got a line of chicks with their bare boobies stickin' out. If you like one of 'em you invite 'em over to your table and afterward they go home with you. And, man, they know how to do it. They got another club there where the chicks sit alone at tables with numbers on 'em. Every table got a telephone. You see a chick you like and you dial her number on the phone and make a date with her. That's real nightclubbin! They know how to do it over there." He pointed to the French girls. "This stuff's too high for my purse."

"Tell 'em about Italy," said Iggy.

"Oh, man, Italy!" moaned Hank. "Four of us went to a house. Real nice girls there. But every time we bought them a drink they brought out a whole bottle. It cost us two hundred and sixty thousand dollars for a piece of Italian pussy."

"Two hundred and sixty thousand dollars!" said Benny.

"We figured it out," said Hank Dixon.

"In Italian dollars," said Iggy. "Two hundred and sixty thousand Italian lira."

Benny laughed. "That's better," he said.

"It was still pretty high," said Hank Dixon. "Over four hundred bucks in American money. We just kept peeling those Italian lira notes off until we didn't have no more."

"We had to walk all the way home," said Iggy. "And after them Italian chicks it wasn't easy."

Wild Man Moore, who had been busy eating and talking to Mr. Seymour, looked up from his plate and said to Eddie, "My boys tell me you're blowin' better'n ever. I gotta come over one night and catch you."

"Any time," said Eddie.

"Yeah," said Mr. Seymour, "your reputation is gettin' better than ever. Your name is really beginnin' to mean somethin' now back in the States thanks to the records you been cuttin'. But there's still nothin' like personal appearances, that's why you ought to come back. 'Course, I don't know how they'd take to the rest of your band . . .."

"Meaning who?" asked Benny angrily.

"Meanin' nothin' personal," replied Mr. Seymour, "except that no matter how you listen to it, jazz is still a colored man's music. We ofays just can't get with it."

"That's a lot of crap and you know it!" said Benny.

"Eddie, I always liked the way you played," said Wild Man. "One of these days we're going to make it together back in the States. You still workin' for Marie?"

"Yeah," replied Eddie.

Wild Man shook his head and made a face. "There's somethin' 'bout that bitch I don't like."

"At least she doesn't take the big cut," said Benny, looking at Mr. Seymour. "It's straight dealin' with her. We don't need no managers."

Mr. Seymour was about to say something but Wild Man beat him to it. "Benny, what the hell you runnin' your mouth off, for? This here dinner is for my honor, for my enjoyment, so you just knock it off and watch what you say, daddy. You hear?"

"He's right," Eddie whispered to Benny, "knock it off."

"Screw him," Benny whispered back.

Eddie knew that normally Benny was not a trouble maker. He wondered whether Benny had ever had a run in with Mr. Seymour before. He asked him.

"Not with him personally," replied Benny, talking low, "but with a dozen vultures like him. They're all the same. Flesh peddlers, that's what they are. I haven't got use for a one of them."

"Well, take it easy; don't get so riled up over it."

"They bring back unpleasant memories. They're blood suckers, vultures, every one of them. Seymour included."

"Hey, is this supposed to be a party or a goddamn conspiracy?" said Wild Man Moore. "Stop mumblin' under your breath," he said to Benny, "and hear me."

"We hear you," said Benny.

"Do you know the one about this French cat who was caught screwin' a dead chick right on the beach . . ."

And so Wild Man Moore began the evening's joke telling. The dirtier they were the more they laughed, even though many of the men had heard most of them before. They told jokes, they ate, they drank, they slapped each other on the back, they asked about friends they hadn't seen in years, they told more jokes.

Eddie was getting annoyed. So this was what Connie wanted to go back to—the joke-telling Americans. Probably the people she hung around with weren't as bad as the jazz musicians, but it was a fact that whenever a group of Americans got together, Negro or white, they felt they had to tell jokes. And they had to laugh hard and loud at them, too.

He was fed up with Wild Man Moore and the rest of them. He was anxious to get back to Connie as soon as he could. He decided that he didn't want to wait until the next morning to get in touch with her. He wanted to see her again that evening. He'd wait until the shindig was a little further under way and then bow out to see her.

"Where the hell is that French cat, Michel the guitar man?" asked Wild Man Moore, looking around at the tables.

"He's in the hospital," said Eddie.

"What's wrong with him?" asked Wild Man.

"I hear he's got the French clap," said Jess Bearden. "Man, that's the worst kind. You better watch yourself, Wild Man, the way you been messin' around!"

They laughed. Eddie tapped the side of his head.

"He flipped?" asked Wild Man.

Eddie nodded yes.

"What's he got to flip for?" asked Hank Dixon. "Man, Europe's the place for us. They know they can't get lovin' from no one like they can from us, and, man they sure are right. He's been livin' here all his life and he flips his lid? Man, he must really be sick!"

Wild Man Moore shook his head. "Man," he said to Hank Dixon, "if you didn't blow such a good horn I wouldn't have nothin' to do with you. Sometimes you are just the stupidest. You think just because a guy can get a piece of white pussy every once in a while all his problems is over."

"What the hell you talkin' about, Wild Man?" said Hank Dixon. "Who the hell is talkin' about white pussy?"

"Then what the hell are you beatin' your chops about?"

"I'm talkin' about *discrimination*. Man, I could see myself flippin' sometimes back in the States. Never mind the South. Man, when we was playin' out in L. A. I used to get stopped by the cops almost every night. Where you goin', they wanna know. For no reason at all, just because I'm colored."

"Your brains is in your ass," said Wild Man. "Everybody gets stopped by the cops in L. A."

"Man," said Hank Dixon, shooting a quick glance at the French girls, "don't you tell me you is as free back home as you is over here."

"Man, I don't know!" said Wild Man Moore. "I don't know what the hell everybody's always beatin' their gums about discrimination for. I play what I wanna play, I goes where I wanna go, nobody ever bothers me. I love everybody and everybody loves me. I don't look for trouble and trouble don't come lookin' for me."

He turned to his manager. "Ain't that right, Mr. Seymour?"

"That's right," said Mr. Seymour. "I say you only find trouble if you go looking for it—like our boy Benny here."

Benny sat up. "And just what do you mean by that?" he asked, his voice pitched unnaturally high.

Some of the other men at the table quieted down. They sensed something was about to happen.

Eddie thought that Benny's attitude toward Mr. Seymour had been uncalled for, considering the occasion. But here was Mr. Seymour starting up with Benny. He was anxious to hear what Mr. Seymour was going to say next. Apparently he hadn't just been sitting there taking Benny's cracks, but had been boiling up inside over them and had finally decided to say something about it.

"You been pickin' on me all night," said Mr. Seymour. "I been keepin' quiet about it 'cause this is a party. But nobody gets away with that noise—not with me they don't. After the party's over you and me are gonna have a few words."

Benny was fuming. "You got anything to say to me you say it right now. Right now!" he demanded.

Mr. Seymour turned to Eddie. "Eddie, what do you keep this bum for? He can't play piano worth a damn. What are you giving him the free ride for?"

Eddie was infuriated by the untruthfulness of the remark as well as its viciousness. He half-rose in his seat. "He's the best goddamned piano man you'll ever hear!"

Wild Man Moore looked up from a piece of roast chicken he was ripping apart with his bare hands and said, "He don't play bad piano."

The other musicians around the table nodded, some rather timidly, afraid of offending Mr. Seymour. Mr. Seymour's face turned red.

"Who cares what he has to say?" yelled Benny. "What the hell does he know about music? What the hell does he know about anything except bloodsucking!"

Wild Man Moore put down his piece of chicken. "All right, Benny, that's enough now. Just shut your face and be a good boy!"

"I'd like to know what you see in him, Wild Man," said Benny. "Everybody knows he's a vulture, a bloodsucker."

Mr. Seymour leaped up and slapped Benny hard across the face. "You sonofabitch!" he screamed. "You get the hell—"

But before he could finish, Benny caught him on the side of his head with a champagne bottle.

Benny wasn't able to get in a full swing and the blow just grazed Mr. Seymour. It was the shock of it rather than the actual blow which knocked him out of the chair.

All of the musicians jumped out of their seats to see what was happening. The two French girls started screaming and one of the waiters ran outside to get the police.

Wild Man Moore started to help Mr. Seymour to his feet. "I'm all right," said Mr. Seymour. "Just get that bastard out of here."

"You could've killed him!" Wild Man Moore screamed at Benny. "What's the matter with you, man!"

"You dirty bastard!" yelled Jess Bearden and he brought his fist down on top of Benny's head. Benny dropped to one knee and Jess was about to hit him again when Eddie punched Jess in the stomach with all his might. As Jess doubled over he reached on the table for a knife. Eddie quickly grabbed the water pitcher and brought it down hard on his hand. He howled in pain. Skinny Sam jumped on Eddie's back and began pummeling him, but Len Smith, Eddie's trumpeter, drove him off by breaking a chair against his back. Another one of Wild Man Moore's boys lunged at Eddie swinging a haymaker, but Eddie ducked and countered with a connecting roundhouse of his own that sent the fellow halfway across the floor. He had put into the blow all the violent disgust he felt at the moment toward Wild Man Moore, his manager, and his boys.

Suddenly it was a wild free-for-all, with most of the men too drunk to know whom they were supposed to be fighting or why and the frantic French waiters staying clear of the whole thing. Bottles began flying all over the place, a table was overturned and Benny, recovering from Bearden's blow, grabbed a tablecloth and threw it over Mr. Seymour, who in the melee had been knocked to the floor again. Mr. Seymour's thrashing wildly about under the tablecloth was appreciated by the men even in the midst of their brawling and gave them an idea.

Silverware, plates, glasses and bottles went flying, cracking, and smashing as cloths were yanked from their tables and flung through the air like sheets in a storm. Wild Man Moore hopped about futilely trying to stop the brawl. The two French girls had managed to make their way to the exit, but just as they were about to escape, the police arrived and the girls were the first ones to get pinched. Police reinforcements were called in but it took a while to break up the riot and get the men to go peace fully into the police wagons.

Wild Man Moore looked back over his shoulder and stared balefully at Eddie.

"A fine dinner party you arranged for me," he called out. "We can't thank you enough, can we, Mr. Seymour?"

But Mr. Seymour paid no attention to what Wild Man Moore said. He was too busy trying to bribe a gendarme not to take them all to jail. It didn't work.

《 15 》

THE MUSICIANS were detained in jail for an hour. Then, after a lecture on civilized behavior, with a gendarme translating into English the remarks of the police official delivering the lecture, they were let out. By this time nobody was talking to anyone else and they all took off on their separate ways.

Eddie returned to his apartment. He felt no remorse at the way the evening had broken up. Instead, he had a feeling of release, almost exhilaration. And he felt proud of Benny for needling Mr. Seymour and starting the ruckus—Benny, who normally was quiet and reserved and looked away from trouble. The one thing he felt sorry about was the forlorn look on Wild Man Moore's face when they were all piled into the police van.

He changed his clothes and went to Connie's hotel. When she didn't answer the house phone he inquired at the front desk. The concierge told him that he had seen Connie and Lillian leave the hotel after dinner but didn't know where they were going or when they would be back.

He sat in the hotel lobby a while, feeling conspicuous and frustrated. He thought that perhaps he should have forced the issue earlier that afternoon. If he had been more persistent he could've got Connie to go to bed with him.

For the first time he realized how much his body ached. There were pains in his neck and back and arms, and the right side of his face felt swollen. He hoped it didn't show too badly. He was very tired but at the same time extremely restless. He had to do something.

He went to the concierge. "When Miss Mitchell returns, would you tell her that . . ." He hesitated.

"Yes?"

"Never mind."

He took a cab to Marie's Cave. It was closed on Sundays. He had a key that let him in through a side door that led to the stairway to Marie's apartment. The door of her apartment was shut. That meant that either she wasn't home or she was entertaining someone, probably Varay. He heard something on the other side of the door. It sounded like the radio. He listened closely. It was a tape recording of Marie singing. He pressed the button on the door and the annoying chimes sounded. He heard the tape recorder clicked off.

Marie opened the door and when she saw Eddie she smiled. She stepped aside so that he could enter the apartment.

Eddie felt nervous and jumpy. He wished Connie had been home when he'd called on her. He wished she had gone to bed with him that afternoon. He half-wished Marie were not home now.

"I heard you singing," he said. He looked at the tape recorder.

"Just fooling around," she said.

"Let's hear it."

"I do it only for my own amusement."

She closed the small spinet and then bent down to put the cover on the tape recorder. She was wearing tight fitting black toreador pants and a low-cut white silk blouse.

"Where's Varay?" Eddie asked.

"Obviously he's not here."

"Do you expect him later?"

"No."

"Are you sure?" Varay was the last person in the world he felt like seeing now.

"He dropped by a little while ago to say good-by. He'll be out of town for a few days."

"Can I have a drink?"

She pointed to the liquor. He poured himself a stiff drink of Scotch.

"I heard about what happened at the Café Francis."

"So soon?"

"That's what you get for messing with Wild Man Moore. He always tries to live up to his reputation."

"It wasn't his fault," said Eddie. "Benny started it all by calling Mr. Seymour a vulture."

"Good for Benny," said Marie. "I didn't think he had it in him."

"Neither did I." He gulped his drink and poured himself another one.

"Give me one, " said Marie, leaning languidly against the spinet.

"Oh, I'm sorry," said Eddie. He poured her a Scotch, handed it to her, lit a cigarette, and nervously paced back and forth.

"Yeah, I don't know what's getting into Benny lately," Eddie went on. "He's been acting funny. All day today. Maybe it's just one of those days. Everybody seems to be flipping. . . . First Michel, then Benny . . ."

"What happened to Michel?" Marie asked.

Eddie told her.

"My God, that's terrible," said Marie. Her obvious concern struck Eddie as strange, especially since she didn't know Michel too well. But then Marie had always been impressed by the fact that Michel was truly a French Negro, one by birth.

"I know he had the reputation for being a little off," she said, "but I never thought he'd crack up. What did he have to crack up about? He's lived in France all his life. It isn't as though he's had to face what we've been through."

"That's right," said Eddie.

Marie sipped her drink and sat on the piano bench. "I'm sure there's quite a difference in the way he was brought up and the way we were brought up. I know his family has money.".

"Yeah," said Eddie, still pacing back and forth, "they're doctors and what-have-you."

"He probably had a governess and went to a private school and played in the parks on the Champs Élysées and spent all his summers in the country. Do you know where I played as a kid? In the cathouse."

Eddie sat down and moved his cigarette back and forth from one hand to the other.

"Oh, I wasn't supposed to be working there, just helping out my Aunt Lucy who was sort of the madam's assistant. I used to run errands for her and clean up around the place and once in a while to amuse the guests I'd sing a song. In fact that's where I started learning to sing."

"Well," said Eddie, "you had to learn someplace." Marie had never told him about her early life back in the States, but what she had just related didn't surprise him. He'd always imagined her early life must have been pretty rough.

"That's where I started learning other things, too. Like the facts of life. I knew what was going on but I wanted to find out what it was first hand, and one day when a hardware salesman asked me to go up to one of the rooms with him I went. I'd heard that making love the way you do when you want to make babies isn't the only way of making love, but I'd never heard of the things he wanted me to do. I told him no, but he twisted my arm in back of me so hard I thought he'd break it and he said he'd kill me if I started to scream, so I had to go ahead and do what he wanted. That was my introduction to the facts of life. I was ten years old at the time."

Eddie knew that he should be shocked, or at least moved, but he wasn't. Perhaps it was because his mind was on other things, on Connie, or wondering whether he was doing the right thing by coming up here and being alone with Marie.

"For weeks after that I couldn't sleep. I had nightmares about it. I used to be afraid the hardware salesman would come back and make me do those things to him again. He never came back. But there were others who were just as bad."

Eddie stood up and crossed to the window.

"What are you jumping up and down for?" asked Marie. "What's bothering you?"

"Nothing's bothering me."

"Then sit down."

"I feel like standing." He lit another cigarette with the butt of the one he was smoking. He crossed the room and put the butt out in an ashtray on top of the piano. He sat down on the edge of the chaise longue.

"You seem a million miles away," said Marie.

"I'm here."

"What are you thinking about?"

"You never told me about being brought up in a cat house," said Eddie.

"There's a lot I never told you. I never told you about my brother Spence, did I?"

"You never told me anything about your family."

"That's because there's nothing worth telling about them. Except Spence. He was the only one I ever liked."

"Where is he now?"

She smiled. "Six feet under."

"Was he an older brother?" He tried to appear interested.

"Younger. I'll never forget the night he came running into the shack with the news that he'd won five dollars. He was so proud. He'd won it in a battle royal. You know what battle royals are, don't you?"

Eddie nodded. A bunch of colored kids are blindfolded and put into a ring. When the bell sounds they start punching and kicking as hard as they can. The one who stays in the longest wins the prize. It used to be a popular form of amusement at white men's clubs in the South.

"His face was all puffed up and bloody, his clothes were torn. But he was so proud he'd won the five dollars. He expected my mother would be happy about it, but instead she beat the hell out of him because he'd almost gotten himself killed. A couple of days later the white store owner my kid brother worked for told him there was going to be another battle royal, but my mother wouldn't let him be in it. The boss taunted my brother, called him a mama's baby, a yellow-bellied nigger, said he'd fire him if he didn't show up for the battle royal.

He showed up. His reputation had preceded him. They put him in the ring with a bunch of older and bigger boys. He had to show them he wasn't a coward. He had to stay in there as long as he could no matter how hard they punched and kicked. At least that's what he told us all, me and my mother and sister. We knew he was hurt bad and we got old Doc Johnson and he tried to save him but he was all busted up inside."

"Jesus," said Eddie.

"I remember my mother saying, 'Hush, boy, you mustn't talk now while the doctor's tendin' you,' and old Doc Johnson saying, 'It's all right. He can talk all he wants to.' I remember I kept asking, 'Is Spence gonna be all right?' but they wouldn't answer me. Two days later he died."

"Jesus," said Eddie. "What'd you do about it?"

"What could we do about it? We were in the good old U. S. A., in the heart of dear old Dixie. Old Doc Johnson made out the death certificate saying the boy had been hit by a truck and nobody dared say otherwise. The next morning we found an envelope at the door with a hundred and fifty dollars in cash. No address on the envelope and no note inside but we knew who it was from. We spent fifty dollars on the funeral and the rest we used to get to New York."

Eddie stared at Marie's long, solid legs. He'd known all along that she must have had good reason to hate America the way she did. He looked up and saw her staring at him. "You can't tell me nothing's bothering you," she said.

He couldn't tell her that it was Connie who was bothering him, Connie and the idea she had planted about his going back to the States.

"Maybe it's you who's bothering me," said Eddie, "you and your lily-white Count."

"Why? You hardly have anything to do with him."

"But you seem to have an awful lot to do with him. Too much, I think. He seems to be moving right in and taking over. Expanding the place . . . telling me what music to play."

"He's always had a financial interest in the club."

"Is that the only reason you've become so friendly with him? For business?"

"Be smart, Eddie, you know Varay. Could there be any other reason?"

"I just can't stand him."

She laughed. "That's wonderful, I didn't know you were jealous."

She crossed to him. Standing over him, she leaned her legs against his.

"You can say what you like about him," said Marie, "but at least he pays some attention to me; at least he knows that I'm alive."

Eddie took Marie's hand. Everything was screwed up. Things were falling away from him. He had to hold on to something. Even if it was something he'd once let go of.

"You'd never think of going back to the States, would you?" he asked.

"Of course not," said Marie. "The biggest mistake I ever made was going back during the war. I loathed it. I'm sure that Paris even under the occupation would've been better."

He put his arms around her thighs and pressed his face against her soft stomach. She ran her hand over his head. "You know," she said, "I've made it a rule never to retrace my steps. But I suppose a rule wouldn't be a rule unless it was broken once in a while."

"We did have some good times together," mumbled Eddie.

"What made you come up all of a sudden?"

"I felt like seeing you."

"Just like that?"

He looked up at her. "You're not sorry I came, are you?"

"No, but I should be getting ready for a party I'm supposed to go to."

"Do you have to go?"

"Not if there's something better to do."

He pulled her down beside him.

Afterward, when Eddie woke up, he noticed that it was but a few minutes to nine. He was in Marie's bed with Marie asleep alongside him. He remembered that he had promised to call Connie but didn't want to call her from Marie's apartment. He quietly got out of bed and started to get dressed.

Marie stirred and woke up.

"Why the rush?" she asked in a lazy drawl. "Come back to bed and rest. You've got a long night ahead of you tonight. Jam session."

"I've an appointment," said Eddie.

"This early in the morning? You must be out of your mind."

"A recording session," he lied.

"Well," she said, "at least give me a good-morning kiss."

He walked back to the bed and kissed her. She held on to him, wanting more than a kiss.

"The recording date's for nine. I'll be late."

"Come back to bed."

"I won't have time."

"The hell with the recording date."

"I better go."

She started to play with him.

"Stop it or I won't be able to get there at all."

He broke away from her and put on his trousers.

"The maid should be here any minute," she said. "We could have breakfast."

"I told you I'm late as it is."

He went into the bathroom and, when he came back, saw Marie propped up in the bed with a quizzical expression on her face.

"Anything wrong?" asked Eddie.

"No."

He put on his shirt and tie. "I hope you don't mind my having to run off like this."

"Will you be able to come back later?"

"Maybe this afternoon, if we finish in time."

He slipped on his jacket.

"One more kiss before you go," she asked.

He kissed her again.

"Such a little one?"

And again.

"That's better."

He finally broke away from her and left the apartment.

Marie decided she'd wait about ten minutes before calling Benny
to find out whether Eddie was really going to a recording session.

##《16》

MARIE, WEARING a white silk dressing gown, was sprawled out on her chaise longue waiting for Benny. Betty, her English maid, puttered around the apartment.

Marie had called Benny and he had revealed that there was no recording session scheduled for that day. She had decided to invite him over for breakfast to try to find out where Eddie had gone.

Whatever his trouble was she was thankful to it for driving him back to her. And now that he was back she intended to make him stay for as long as she could. Last night had been fun.

Not like with Varay. She had to laugh to herself when she thought of Varay. The French were supposed to be such great lovers! Varay looked distinguished and sophisticated and certainly all-knowing about women. But in bed he was impetuous and uncontrolled—like a little boy. Sometimes he even trembled. Not with any great passion. It was more like a little firecracker going off. Once and he was finished for the evening—finished for the week! He'd lie there with a stupid smirk on his face, as if he'd made a great conquest, as though he'd satisfied the Queen of Sheba. And she'd stroke his fevered forehead, pretending that he was such a wonderful lover, although he had never satisfied her once, not once.

But Varay did have more money than any man she knew.

She went over to her closet, opened it and gazed at herself in the full-length mirror. White always did make her look stouter but she knew it wasn't wearing white that made her look stout now. She ran her hands over her hips. There was no doubt about it—she was developing a spread. She was never exactly what one would call slim but she was never as broad in the beam as she was at present. Well, she thought, there's no holding back the clock, is there?

The door chimes sounded. She returned to the chaise longue, got into a comfortable position and gave her maid the signal to open the door.

Benny entered wearing a Band-aid on his forehead.

She had never liked Benny and was aware that the feeling was somewhat mutual. She could never understand Eddie's friendship for the short, plump man; certainly she never approved of it.

Benny crossed the room and, clicking his heels together and bowing like a German officer in an old fashioned movie, kissed her hand.

The fool, thought Marie. She hated his clowning, but concealed her anger.

"How are you, Benny? It's been a long time since we've had a chat."

"I don't think we've ever had what you call 'a chat,' " said Benny, imitating Marie's slight continental accent.

"Would you like some chocolate for breakfast or would you prefer coffee?"

"Do you have American coffee?" asked Benny.

"No."

"Well, let's see . . . I guess I'll suffer through some café au lait."

"Would you like an omelet or something like that?"

"Coffee and croissants will be fine."

Marie gave the order to her maid, who left for the kitchen to prepare it. The table was already set and Marie walked over to it. When Benny held the chair out for her he again clicked his heels. Always the clown, always the fool, thought Marie, but all she said was, "Thank you."

The maid was prompt with the breakfast, and Marie tried to keep her annoyance from showing when Benny dipped the croissant into the coffee as if it were a dough nut. She felt that he was doing this just to annoy her.

"I heard about what happened last night," she said.

"Yeah," said Benny, his mouth full of coffee-soaked croissant. He pointed to his Band-aid.

"I would wear that as a badge of honor," Marie said. "I've always hated that son-of-a-bitch Mr. Seymour. To tell you the truth I find Wild Man Moore pretty disgusting, too."

"I thought the two of you were friends."

"I've known him since New Orleans, if that's what you mean. He hasn't changed one bit. He's still the same primitive ape he always was."

Benny didn't answer. She sensed he wanted to drop the small talk.

"I suppose you're wondering why I asked you up here."

"I know it isn't because you can't resist my charms." He winked at her.

She hated his guts. "I want to talk to you about something of mutual interest to us."

"What's that?"

"Eddie."

He looked up at her puzzled. "Shoot."

She sipped her chocolate. "He came up to see me last night. He seemed—"

"You're kidding," interrupted Benny. "Eddie came up here?"

"That's right," said Marie. "And he seemed terribly upset."

Benny pointed to his Band-aid.

"It wasn't the brawl," said Marie. "It was something else."

"Go on."

"I thought you might know what it was."

"How the hell should I know? I wasn't with him last night. You were. Why didn't you ask him."

Benny had a chip on his shoulder. No one ever talked that way to her. She felt like throwing him the hell out. But first she had to find out about Eddie.

"I did ask him," she replied. "He wouldn't tell me."

"Maybe he was constipated."

"He's not the same old Eddie."

"He seems like the same old Eddie to me," said Benny. "I don't know what the hell you're talking about."

There was no doubt in Marie's mind that Benny knew what she meant. He was too close to Eddie not to notice the change taking place in him.

"I told you that he was here last night," said Marie. "I couldn't help noticing he was worried. He's got something on his mind."

"We all have things on our minds from time to time, don't we?"

"This was different."

"Maybe he's going through a change of life. It happens with men, too, you know."

She saw that Benny just didn't intend to open up. Not to this direct approach, anyway.

"If something did happen to Eddie," said Marie, "it would affect us both quite a bit. The club would be losing its main attraction, one of the best jazzmen in Paris, and I suppose you'd be losing a job."

Benny poured himself another cup of coffee. "What could happen to Eddie?" he asked. "If he quit the club I'm sure he'd take me with him. He always has in the past. Where he goes I go. That's how it's always been."

The maid asked Marie if there was anything else she wanted. Marie dismissed her with a shake of the hand.

"What if he were to go back to the States?" asked Marie.

"Oh, he'd never do that."

"Are you sure?"

"What makes you think that he would?"

"Look, Benny, I've been here a lot longer than you. I've seen them when they first come over with looks of wonder and excitement in their faces. I've seen them when they've been here a while looking relaxed and con tented and blasé and taking everything in their stride. And I've seen them with that troubled look that means only one thing—they're ready to go back."

"And you think that's the case with Eddie?"

"I saw that look on him last night."

Benny drained his cup of coffee. "It's funny his coming up here last night. I thought it was all over between the two of you."

Marie smiled. "I would say we've never been closer."

"He must be an awfully good man, especially since I know for a fact how much time he's been spending in the last couple of days with Connie."

"Who's she?"

Benny wiped his lips with his napkin. "She's the one who makes it hard for me to believe that there's still anything between you and Eddie."

"Is she white?"

"What difference does that make?"

"Is she an American?"

"Yeah."

Marie frowned.

"She's a helluva nice girl. I've never seen him in so deep with any dame before. I think he's really hooked this time."

She felt that he was saying it just to get her goat. Any way she'd found out what she wanted to know. "Was it the girl he went out with Saturday night?"

"Sunday, too."

"But yet he came to see me last night. How interested could he be in her?"

"Well, don't take my word for it. Why don't you get it right from the horse's mouth. Or, if you wait a few days, you'll probably get an announcement . . . maybe an invitation to the wedding." He laughed.

Marie jerked her chair back from the table and returned to the chaise longue. "We've got to work together on this. We'll both work on him. And we'll have to work on the girl, too."

Benny threw his napkin on the table and crossed to the piano stool. "Why the hell should we interfere?"

"Because his stupid infatuation with this girl may be the reason he wants to return to the States."

"That's his business."

"It's our business, too. It's the worst thing that could happen to him. You know how he'd regret it later on."

"That's not for us to decide."

"Would you want him to go back to the States?"

"Not particularly."

"Well . . ."

She motioned to him with her hand. "Benny, come here a moment."

He walked toward her.

"Sit down." She made room for him to sit down next to her on the chaise longue.

"I want you to bring this girl up to see me." She put her hand on Benny's arm.

"Lay off!" Benny said sharply. He jumped up. "No, I'll be damned if I'm going to interfere. And you better not either!"

Marie sat up. "But we both agree that it would be bad for him to go back."

"I don't agree to nothing!"

"For Eddie's own good . . ."

"Don't you pretend you have Eddie's own good in mind. You know you have no one's good in mind but Marie Le Brun's. It's always been that way and always will be that way. If Eddie is really thinking of going back that's his business and we've got no right interfering. So you lay off me and lay off him!"

"Don't you use that tone of voice with me!" Marie screamed. "Don't you tell me what to do or what not to do!"

The maid appeared from the kitchen to see what all the yelling was about.

"Open the door for him," said Marie. "He's leaving." The maid held open the door.

"Now get out!" Marie shouted.

"Screw you!" said Benny as he left.

The maid closed the door after him.

"Dirty Jew bastard," Marie mumbled under her breath.

#《17》

AFTER EDDIE had left Marie's apartment he had gone to the nearest restaurant that had a public phone. He took a telephone token out of his pocket, lifted the telephone receiver off the hook and then changed his mind. He put back the receiver, sat down at a small table against the wall and ordered breakfast.

He knew that Connie was waiting for his call but he suddenly felt peculiar about calling her.

It would lead nowhere. They were from two entirely different worlds. A jazz musician and a schoolteacher. It didn't make sense. It would never work out. He'd lived too long in Paris. He couldn't go back to the States.

Besides, there was still Marie. How much could he care for Connie if he had run back to Marie? No, the best thing to do was to forget about Connie. He'd see her once more to say good-by. He did owe her at least that.

He finished eating and paid his check. He decided to call her but he'd wait a while first. Perhaps she'd already taken off for the Musée d'Art Moderne and wouldn't be in anyway. Then he'd reach her in the evening. There was no rush.

He walked along the Seine, looked at some books and prints at the bookstalls, looked at some of the small boats passing down the river, looked at the French people at work, looked at the tourists armed with cameras and guidebooks marching briskly to their cultural destinations, sat on a bench and glanced through a French newspaper. There was no mention in the newspaper of the fight the night before at the Café Francis. When he couldn't sit any longer he hurriedly entered a phone booth and nervously called Connie.

He was half-hoping that she wasn't in, but she was.

"I didn't go to the museum," she explained. "I told them I wasn't feeling well. You said that you would call at nine."

"I'm sorry," he said, "but . . ." He couldn't think of any excuse. "Can I pick you up now?" He was glad that his voice sounded calm.

"Sure. I'll wait for you downstairs in the lobby."

He hung up and quickly walked to the Metro. His throat felt dry.

Connie was waiting for him just inside the entrance to the hotel. She was wearing the same tan outfit she had on when he first met her. She looked wonderful.

"Have you had breakfast?"

"Yes."

"Any place you'd like to go?"

"Makes no difference to me. Any place you say. Except the Musée d'Art Moderne. It would be embarrassing to meet the other teachers there after I told them I wasn't feeling well. Why don't we just walk? Or are you tired after yesterday?"

"No, I'm fine," he said.

They started down the street.

He wondered whether he should tell her right now. But tell her what? Connie, I hope you're not getting any wrong ideas? Connie, I hope I'm not misleading you? Connie, I really didn't mean some of the things I said yesterday?

"Connie, I . . ."

"Yes?"

"There's something I wanted to say to you."

"Yes?"

He hesitated. How to begin?

"I—well, I'll tell you later."

"What is it?"

"I—it's nothing! It's not important. Never mind."

"Now you've really got my curiosity up."

"Forget it. How would you like to go over to the Cirque d'Hiver? Some friends of mine are making a movie there and it might be fun to watch for a while."

"Anything you say."

She hooked her arm in his. Eddie wondered what Marie would think if she saw the two of them together. The whole thing was weird. One moment making a play for Connie and being turned down by her, the next moment in bed with Marie, and right after that back to Connie again. But this time it was just to say good-by.

"Watch it!" Connie said. They quickly stepped back on the curb to avoid being hit by a speeding automobile.

"The way they drive in this town!" said Connie.

They crossed the street.

Connie said, "The concierge told me that a young man was at the hotel last night to see me. That must've been you."

"That's right. I dropped by."

"I had no idea you were going to or I would've waited for you. Lillian and I went to a movie on the Champs Élysées."

"What'd you see?"

"Some American movie. I forget the name of it. It was funny but I couldn't follow it. I expected to see French titles, you know, the way we put English titles on foreign movies. But instead, Jane Russell and all of the other American actors came out speaking French. We couldn't understand a word."

"Yes, that's what they do to practically all the American movies—they dub them."

"What did you do last night?" asked Connie.

"Nothing much. Some of the boys gave a dinner for Wild Man Moore."

"Didn't you go?"

"Yes, I went."

"When did you drop by to see me?"

"Afterwards."

"Oh. And then what did you do after you didn't find me in?"

"Nothing . . ."

"Just listen to me!" she exclaimed self-critically. "How nosey I'm getting!"

After about an hour of walking both Connie and Eddie agreed that it would be best to take a cab the rest of the way to the Cirque d'Hiver.

Connie didn't know that the Cirque d'Hiver was a circus. The circus show itself was over for the season but a French film company was using the site and circus personnel for part of a motion picture.

Eddie introduced Connie to the many people he knew, both in the circus itself and in the film company, and saw that she was duly impressed. They were all glad to see him, as he knew they would be.

He and Connie sat down in one of the stands and watched the filming. It was the first movie Connie had ever seen being made and while she was obviously interested in it, Eddie caught her several times looking at him rather than at what was happening before the cameras.

"It's interesting, isn't it?" he asked.

"Yes, very."

But it was clear to him how much more she was interested in him than in the movie.

"We can leave any time you want to," he said.

"Any time you say."

"They'll be breaking in a little while for lunch. We could go out and have a bite with them. Might be interesting.

"Anything you say."

"They're a bunch of characters."

When it was time for lunch they joined Eddie's friends at a little restaurant nearby that was frequented by circus performers. It was alive and colorful and noisy. Clowns in full costume and makeup, midgets, roustabouts, animal trainers and jugglers were there. It was no place for a quiet conversation. It was no place to say good-by.

As they sat and talked and joked with the movie and circus people Eddie thought that perhaps he was making too much of the whole thing. Connie would be leaving Paris in a few days. Why not let it all peter out by itself? Why bring it to a head now? What the hell, this was probably no more than a summer romance for her, a schoolteacher's adventure in Paris. That's all it probably meant to her. Once back in the States she'd be glad it hadn't gone any further than that.

The atmosphere of the tiny restaurant was completely unreal to Eddie. He'd been there before and now, as in the previous times, it was like being in an entirely different world, one completely removed from the life he knew, from reality, from problems. It was no place even to think about serious things.

"Waiter! Wine for everybody!" he ordered. "And quick!"

"Hey! What's the occasion?" asked Meta, a bareback rider.

"He must be celebrating," said Bojo, a clown, "because he's in love." He looked at Connie, made a heartsick face and fluttered his eyelids.

They all laughed.

"Where's the waiter?" asked the production manager.

"We'll have to break this up soon and get back to start shooting again."

"The killjoy!" shouted Meta.

The others good-naturedly booed and hissed the production manager.

The waiter came with the wine and, finally, it was time to return to the set. Eddie and Connie were invited to watch the afternoon's work.

They all started walking back toward the circus. Eddie and Connie lingered slightly behind the others.

"What do you say?" asked Eddie. "Would you like to go back and see some more shooting?"

"It's fine with me—unless there's some place else you'd like to go."

Eddie knew there would be little chance to talk on the set. They had to remain silent while the shooting was going on.

"Let's go back," he said. "We can leave in a little while if we want to."

They went back inside.

The movie being made at the Cirque d'Hiver was a hackneyed and banal circus story. The circus performers were used merely for background color. The actors in the film were obviously only adequate, the director was unimaginative and, all in all, Eddie felt the entire operation boring. But he pretended he was interested and he remained there with Connie until late in the afternoon when the shooting was halted.

The director invited them to join him for cocktails.

"I have to get back to the hotel," said Connie.

"Oh come, my dear, you can take time off for a drink," persisted the director.

"I'm sorry, but I have to get back."

"Eddie . . ." appealed the director.

"We'll make it some other time," said Eddie. He opened the door of a cab and Connie got inside. He told the cab driver the name of the hotel.

After they'd ridden in silence a while Eddie asked, "Why didn't you want to go with him for a drink?"

"I felt like being alone with you. You said before you had something you wanted to tell me."

"Oh, it was nothing."

"Come on."

"I forgot what it was," said Eddie. "It couldn't have been very important."

"I think you're not telling the truth," said Connie. "You remember. You've just changed your mind about telling me."

"And if I have changed my mind? I can do that, can't I? You're not going to force me to tell you, are you?"

"See if I care!" she pouted playfully. Then, smiling, she rested her head on Eddie's shoulder. Eddie put his arm around her.

They stepped out of the cab in front of her hotel and Eddie took her hand and said, "I hope you'll be able to make it over to the club later for the jam session."

"I don't see why not," said Connie, "if you really want me there."

"Of course I do. Would you want me to pick you up and bring you over?"

"No, I'll get there later. I've some cards I want to send."

Suddenly, down the street, appeared Mrs. Vogel and her charges on their way back from the museum.

"Good afternoon, Connie," said Mrs. Vogel. And she added sarcastically, "I'm glad to see that you're feeling much better."

Some of the teachers giggled. Lillian, who was walking with Martin Weiner, waved hello cheerfully to Eddie. Mrs. Vogel led them into the hotel.

"I'll see you later tonight then," said Eddie.

❰❰18❱❱

ANOTHER MONDAY night. Another jam session. There were, as usual: the kids of the bourgeoisie out to be unbourgeois, some wearing beards and turtleneck sweaters, and their girls with too much make-up or not enough; the odd-faced Saint-Germain-des-Prés kids who somehow had got enough money for the one drink they had to buy to stay at Marie's Cave; the forever faithful French followers of any and all jazz, who had taken to it when it first hit Europe in the Twenties when they were in their twenties; the cold intellectuals; the American expatriates; the American students; the small groups of American tourists entering and leaving as part of the Paris-By-Night tours; the visiting jazz musicians waiting for their turn to play.

It was early in the evening. The band had got off to an early start. Sparked by Eddie, they played with unusual imagination and dexterity, each man making the most of his riff. But it was Eddie who played with outstanding brilliance. And when he played a blues he poured into it all of his loneliness and quiet despair, his sense of futility. He wasn't good at verbalizing what he felt, not the subtler, more complex feelings. But he could express himself in his music.

He hadn't expressed himself this way in too long a time. But he was doing it now. And they all knew he was doing it. They got the message.

So did Connie when she wandered into the club, and so did Lillian and Martin Weiner, who came in with her.

They, too, got the message.

Eddie knew Connie would come, although he didn't expect her to come with friends. He nodded hello to her while he continued to play.

And someone else got the message, too. Someone he didn't expect to see. Not after last night. An extra added attraction at Marie's Cave, their greatest possible extra added attraction. Gleeful whisperings to the others by those who spotted him first, and all heads turned around, and all faces with broad smiles of joyous anticipation. Into Marie's Cave walked Wild Man Moore. Perhaps the great one would sit in with the boys and then they'd really hear something!

Accompanying Wild Man Moore was Mr. Seymour. Eddie glanced at Benny and saw the worried look on Benny's face, as though he was expecting trouble.

Wild Man Moore and his manager sat poker-faced, Wild Man all eyes and ears for Eddie. Obviously they hadn't come to start any trouble. When some well-wishers gathered around Wild Man Moore, he politely brushed them off so he could concentrate on Eddie's playing.

Eddie finished the set. It was time for some of the other musicians to sit in. They started pure Dixieland with hopes of enticing Wild Man Moore to join them.

Mr. Seymour motioned to Eddie to come over. "Sit down," said Mr. Seymour.

"I've some friends waiting for me at the other table," replied Eddie.

"Sit down, daddy," said Wild Man. Eddie sat down, motioning to Connie that he'd be over in a minute.

Benny passed by without bothering to look at Wild Man Moore or Mr. Seymour and sat down at Connie's table.

A few more well-wishers and admirers came over to greet Wild Man Moore. He spoke to them as briefly as possible, making it plain that he wasn't in a party mood.

"Man, is there some place we can talk?" he asked Eddie.

"What's wrong with here?" said Eddie.

"I mean private."

Eddie didn't say anything. He wondered what Wild Man Moore wanted to speak to him about. He wondered if it had anything to do with last night.

As though in answer to Eddie's thoughts Wild Man Moore said, "Man, that was some workout we had last night."

"It's a lucky thing nobody got hurt," added Mr. Seymour. He shot a glance in Benny's direction. "You've got an awfully fresh boy," he said.

"I don't seem to remember that he was the one who started the swinging," said Eddie.

"At least I didn't pick up no bottle," said Mr. Seymour.

"All that jazz is ancient history now," said Wild Man. He tilted his head and looked at Eddie and like a father giving his son advice added, "But, Eddie, daddy, you shouldn't have brought that water pitcher down on Bearden's hand so hard. As a musician yourself you should know better'n to mess with another musician's hands."

"I'm sorry about that," said Eddie. "But he was reaching for a knife. Anyway, I didn't hurt him, did I?"

"Only one finger," said Wild Man Moore. "Don't worry none about it. It won't interfere with his playin'. He'll just have to lay off stink finger a while, that's all." He laughed loudly.

Eddie had to laugh too.

"Catch him now! Catch him now!" said Wild Man Moore to Mr. Seymour. "He laughed! The saddest man in all Paris actually laughed!"

"You going to sit in with the boys later?" asked Eddie.

"Man, what do you want from me," exclaimed Wild Man. "This here's my night off. Look, ain't there some place where we can be alone? Just the two of us?"

The idea of losing Mr. Seymour for a while appealed to Eddie. He wondered whether Marie was upstairs. He still carried a key to her apartment, even though he hadn't used it in years. He didn't think she'd mind his making use of her place when she wasn't there.

He turned his head around and saw that Connie was staring at him. He wanted to speak to her before going up with Wild Man Moore.

He excused himself for a moment and went over to the table. Connie introduced him to Martin Weiner.

"Won't you sit down and join us?" asked Lillian. She seemed especially glad to see Eddie.

"I can't just now," said Eddie. "Wild Man Moore wants to see me about something. I'll be back in a little while, though."

"Good," said Connie. "We'll be waiting for you." In the reflection of candle light she appeared to Eddie more beautiful than ever.

He went back to Wild Man Moore and Mr. Seymour. They were huddled in frantic conference. They quickly stopped when Eddie approached.

"I think I know where we can go," said Eddie.

"Lead the way," said Wild Man Moore.

Mr. Seymour stood up as though to join them.

"I thought you said just the two of us," said Eddie.

"We're just gonna talk," said Wild Man Moore to Mr. Seymour.

Mr. Seymour gave in. He sat down. "All right. I'll be waiting for you here."

A howl of protest went up as Eddie and Wild Man Moore made their way toward the door.

"Don't worry," shouted Wild Man Moore, "I'll be back! I'm comin' right back!" He gave them the famous Wild Man Moore cry and they roared in appreciation.

As they climbed the stairs to the apartment Wild Man Moore said, "I know nobody digs Mr. Seymour. Sometimes I don't dig him myself. But he sure digs me and, man, that's important, especially on the road. You gotta have a guy like that around, man, no matter how the cats feel about him."

As they reached the landing at the top of the stairs, the door of Marie's apartment swung open. Varay stood in the doorway, Marie behind him. Varay was obviously on his way out. Eddie and Varay greeted each other and Eddie introduced him to Wild Man Moore.

"Of course I know the fabulous Wild Man Moore," said Varay. "I had the extreme pleasure of attending your concert last week. What a shame that I must be off now. If Eddie had informed me in advance that he was going to bring you here this evening I would have rearranged my appointments to be able to spend some time with you."

Wild Man Moore looked beyond Varay's shoulder and saw Marie. He waved to her. "Hiyah, doll!"

She smiled back feebly.

Varay looked at his watch. "Perhaps I can be a few minutes late," he said. He ushered Eddie and Wild Man Moore into the apartment.

"Actually," said Eddie, "we didn't come up here to socialize. We were looking for a quiet place where the two of us could talk alone."

Varay's lips tightened. "Well in that case I suppose I can leave right on schedule. Nice to have met you, Mr. Moore."

"Same here, daddy," said Wild Man Moore.

"I shall see you tomorrow," said Varay to Marie, and he left the apartment.

Marie and Wild Man Moore faced each other. "It's been a long time, doll," said Wild Man Moore.

"Yes, I suppose it has," answered Marie.

"You haven't changed since the last time I seen you," said Wild Man Moore. "Still as good-lookin' as ever. Man, this here Paris life must agree with you."

"How have you been?" asked Marie coldly.

"Oh, you know we've been travelin'! Man, we've been all over the world!"

"Really?" said Marie. "That's nice."

"Come on, daddy," said Wild Man Moore to Eddie. "Let's you and me find our quiet place."

"You can stay here if you want to," said Marie, sharply. "I've something to do inside anyway." She went into the bedroom and slammed the door.

"Speak about cold how-do-you-do's," said Wild Man Moore. "That Marie-chick's reception could freeze a fish. Let's shake this joint." He started for the door.

"Wait a second," said Eddie. "Don't worry about her. We can talk here. Sit down."

Wild Man Moore sat down on a chair. Eddie sat down on the couch. Wild Man Moore jumped up and sat down on the couch next to him. "I better talk low," Wild Man Moore whispered, "'cause I don't want that bitch to hear what I gotta say."

"You don't have to whisper," said Eddie. "I'm sure she's not listening at the door."

"If she knew what I wanted to speak to you about she'd have a fit," said Wild Man Moore, continuing to whisper. "Maybe I ought to speak up," he said, smiling diabolically. "But I don't wanna make no trouble for you. Anyway, what I came here to ask you is if you ain't tired yet of this French bit, 'cause if you is, and you wanna come back to the States, yours truly would like nothin' better than for you to be blowin' in his new little combo. One or two of the boys are droppin' out by request after the trip we're now on is done with and, man, hearin' you blow just now shows me that what I been hearin' about you these last couple of years has been exaggerated the other way. By that I mean the raves ain't been big enough. Man, you is the greatest!"

Eddie was flattered. A compliment from Wild Man Moore wasn't to be taken lightly. "Why thanks, Wild Man," he said. "Thanks a lot."

"Whatya think?"

"I'm afraid I must say no. I wasn't planning to return to the States."

"Hell, what're you gonna do, man, settle down here for the rest of your life?"

"I wasn't planning on coming back yet," said Eddie.

"Man, you've been over here a helluva long time." Eddie didn't answer.

"Maybe you don't like the idea of giving up your own band?" asked Wild Man Moore.

"Well, that's part of it. But I was thinking about that. I thought that after that fight last night . . ."

"Hell, like I said before, that's all old jazz now! The only thing I care about right now is the way you blow that horn. Of course, you wouldn't be able to bring your boy Benny along into the outfit. Man, Mr. Seymour don't interfere with who I wants in the band, but I sure do think he'd put his foot down on that cat."

Eddie stood up. "As I said, I appreciate your offer. I feel flattered. But I'm afraid the answer is no."

"Well," said Wild Man Moore, still whispering, "I think it's a shame wastin' the way you blow over here. Like I told you, you could make a mint back in the States, even if you don't wanna be part of my band. You think about it. Any time you're ready I'll make room for you. And when you're ready to talk business, come see Mr. Seymour. That's his department. But don't worry about that. We'll see that you're happy."

"I like it here in Paris," said Eddie.

Wild Man Moore shrugged his shoulders. "Just thought I'd speak to you," he said. "Let's go downstairs. I'll buy you a drink."

Wild Man Moore crossed to Marie's bedroom. He rapped on the door, opened it a few inches, and called inside, "We're leaving, Marie!"

There was no response. Wild Man Moore gave his cry and Eddie heard Marie yelp in fright. Wild Man laughed and closed the door. The two of them went back down stairs to the club.

As soon as they saw Wild Man Moore reappear the crowd pleaded with him to play for them. He borrowed a trumpet from one of the boys in the band and, after a brief consultation with them on what he was going to play, took off on *The Down Home Rag.*

Eddie went over to Connie's table.

"Boy, he sure is great," said Martin Weiner.

"He's good and loud anyway," said Lillian.

After the number the crowd broke into wild cheers and applause. Wild Man Moore quieted them down by waving his hands. Then he pointed to Eddie and indicated that he should join him up on the bandstand. The crowd voiced their hearty approval.

And the two of them played together. They played *Tin Roof Blues* and *Panama and Careless Love Blues.* The way they played complemented each other and the crowd loved it. Then, somehow, nobody was aware how it started, they began a cutting contest, each trying to out-do the other.

Whatever song it was they started out with, perhaps it was *Sister Kate,* was soon submerged in melodic improvisations. Each man blew for all he was worth, trying to top the other.

The crowd went wild.

News of what was happening leaped from table to table and spread to other clubs up and down the street. In a matter of minutes Marie's Cave was jammed to capacity.

The air was so filled with cigarette smoke that the candles atop the tables seemed to flicker from lack of oxygen, illuminating faces grotesquely frozen in hypnotic attentiveness.

While they played nobody talked. Then when each man finished his solo the crowd would break into deafening applause and shout themselves hoarse until the other man picked up the solo. Then silence fell and the packed crowd strained forward to hear, listening to each man give his interpretation of the same song.

Slowly, some of the men from Wild Man Moore's band gathered together and began to back their boss. On the other part of the bandstand gathered the boys from Eddie's band. No longer was it a cutting contest just between the two men. Now it was a battle between the two bands, with each leader sparking his men and inspiring them by example to do things they had never done before.

From the street people kept pouring into the club until it was impossible to squeeze in another soul. They packed the space between tables, overflowed up the steps and into the street outside. Marie came down and observed behind the safety of the door that led to her apartment. Many of the people lucky enough to have chairs shared them with others.

Lillian, before she was aware of what was happening, found herself sitting on the lap of a bearded bohemian.

On and on the men played, louder, wilder, more brilliantly— sweating, short of breath, exhausted and exhilarated. A commotion arose in the rear of the club when two photographers from *Paris Match* battled their way just inside the entrance but were allowed to go no further. Holding their cameras as high up in the air as they could to shoot above the heads of the crowd, they took their pictures. Everyone except Lillian was too caught up in the music to pay any attention to the flashbulbs popping off. Lillian hoped that she would be in one of the pictures. It would cause quite a stir when she showed it at school.

After almost two hours of uninterrupted battling, both bands got together on *When the Saints Come Marching In*, and when the last note of the song was sounded, that was it. The musicians had had it. Even the people in the club were too exhausted to ask for more. The men who twenty-four hours earlier had been fighting one another now threw their arms around each other and insisted on buying the drinks.

Other musicians who had not had their chance to play timidly took over on the stand but they knew that what they were going to play would now sound about as exciting as Guy Lombardo.

Both Eddie and Wild Man Moore were mobbed by the worshiping hand-shakers and back-slappers.

Marie wormed her way through the crowd to Connie. "Excuse me," she asked, "but are you waiting for Eddie?"

Connie was surprised. "Me?"

"You're Connie, aren't you?"

"Yes."

"I thought I recognized you. You were here Saturday night, weren't you?"

"That's right."

"Could you come with me now for a few minutes? My apartment is above the club."

Connie hesitated. "Just for a moment," said Marie, and taking Connie by the hand led her through the crowds to the door that led to her apartment.

Marie closed the door behind her, told Connie to sit down and offered her a drink, which Connie refused. Marie sat down opposite her.

"Relax, child," said Marie. "You look so nervous and ill at ease. I promise I'm not going to bite you."

"It's just that . . . I didn't expect this. I mean . . ."

"Do you know who I am?"

"I assume that you're Marie."

"Is that all you know about me?"

"Why—yes."

Marie laughed. "You're very cute. And very naive. You don't know it but right now I also happen to be a very good friend of yours. I'm going to save you from having a lot of heartache later on. Oh, I admit that I'm not acting for completely unselfish reasons. I'm so tired of the scenes Eddie's sweet little things make when they find out that I'm the only one who really matters in his life. I thought before things get more complicated I'd save us both some embarrassment later on."

Connie stopped her nervous fidgeting. She knew that Eddie was no saint. She knew that he was probably involved with a lot of women.

But she had no idea that there was that certain one woman in his life. Not with all the time and attention he had given her during the past few days.

"I'm afraid I don't know what you mean," Connie said.

"Come now," said Marie, "let's be realistic about this. I know exactly how much time you've spent with him over the weekend. It's been considerable, except, of course, for last night, which he spent sleeping with me."

Connie was speechless.

"I'm not particularly upset about it," said Marie. "Not after all these years. As a matter of fact, I've sort of gotten used to it. I know that Eddie has to digress once in a while if only to appreciate me all the more. It's just that every once in a while I get to feeling sorry for his innocent little playmates. And I do hate those scenes that sometimes come up later on."

It couldn't be true, thought Connie. All the time they had spent together, the things they had enjoyed, shared, even the things they had bickered, argued and fought about—it couldn't all have been just a front, just a build-up to a quick affair.

"Maybe Eddie has the feeling that these little side trips add spice to our own romance—which has been going on for more years that I'd care to admit. Anyway, out of consideration for both of us and, I suppose, for Eddie's own good, too, I thought I'd tell you what the situation was."

Marie looked Connie over carefully.

"I must admit that you're one of the nicest ones he's gotten involved with."

"How did you know about me?" asked Connie. "Did Eddie tell you?"

"We were together all evening. We did talk part of the time. After all, considering all the years we've known one another, we do take time out every once in a while for talk."

Connie stood up. "I find this all very embarrassing and unnecessary. I don't know what you think and I don't particularly care, but there's absolutely nothing between Eddie and me. How could there be? We've only known each other a few days. It's true that he's spent some time with me, that he's shown me around Paris, but that's all there's to it."

"Believe me, child," said Marie, smiling knowingly, "if I didn't know there was more to it than that I wouldn't have invited you up here. I know the kind of devil that Eddie is. I suppose that's one of the reasons I love him the way I do. And because I'm as understanding as I am I suppose that's one of the reasons he loves me."

"Well it so happens that this is one time you're completely wrong," said Connie.

She crossed to the door and angrily pulled it open. "Maybe if there was any real love between the two of you he wouldn't carry on the way he does. Did you ever think of that?" She strode out, slamming the door behind her.

Marie relaxed. She felt she had done her work well. But of course in these things you could never know for sure.

It was only when Wild Man Moore was finally dragged away by Mr. Seymour that the crowd began to thin out at Marie's Cave and Eddie was able to get away from his fans to see Connie. He was surprised and disappointed to find that she and her party had gone. Benny was seated at the table with some of his friends.

"I guess she got tired of hanging around," said Eddie.

"Tired? Hell, no!" explained Benny. "She was raging mad about something. She left in a hurry, dragging Lillian and the boy with her. It's a shame, because I wanted to hear what Lillian had to say about the music."

«19»

"THREE MORE days and then good-by to Paris," said Lillian. She opened her valise and took out a dark gray cardigan. "It seems to be a bit cooler this morning," she said, holding the cardigan at arm's length and shaking it out. She put it on, looked in the mirror and said, "It is a dull color, though, isn't it?"

Connie, seated at the small desk writing cards to her students, looked up. "It's all right."

Lillian tied a blue scarf around her neck. "There, that gives me a bit of color."

Connie wasn't in the mood for sending postcards, but she had to do something. She was distraught over last night's meeting with Marie, had spent a sleepless night and now felt that it would be best to get her mind on other things.

She remembered that the student she was writing to had a new bicycle. *Dear Alvin, she wrote. You would certainly feel at home here with your new bicycle. Cycling in France is not only a favorite pastime with the boys and girls, but with the grown-ups as well. I hope you are having fun on your summer vacation. Sincerely, Miss Mitchell.*

"The plans for this morning are to visit the Galeries Lafayette and the Au Printemps," said Lillian. "They're two of the leading department stores in Paris."

"That should be interesting," said Connie glumly.

"You make it sound as though it will be the most boring thing in the world."

Dear Amy, wrote Connie, *I thought of you when we visited the Versailles Gardens, for I know how much you like flowers . . .* She put her pen down.

189

"It's just that I'm tired," she said. "I didn't sleep very well last night."

"I know," said Lillian. "I heard you tossing and turning."

"I'm sorry if it annoyed you," said Connie.

Lillian put her valise back into the closet. "I think you ought to call Eddie," she said.

"After all I told you?"

Lillian looked at her watch. "We don't have to be down in the lobby for another fifteen minutes. Why don't you call him now? I'll leave."

"No," said Connie, sharply. She stood up and started to pace slowly around the room. Lillian sat down in the corner chair and watched her.

"I know it's foolish of me to feel this way," said Connie. "He means nothing to me. It's just that I suppose I'm somewhat disappointed."

"I don't know why you're taking what that woman said as the truth," said Lillian.

"What reason would she have to lie to me?"

"Jealousy."

"How did she know about me? Eddie must have told her."

"But you don't know *what* he told her. He may have told her what a nice girl he thought you were, how much he liked you. That's what may have made her jealous."

Connie stood still and shook her head.

"She may have made up those things she told you about herself and Eddie," said Lillian. "At any rate I think you owe Eddie a chance to explain. To be fair you should get his side of the story."

"I have an uneasy feeling that she was telling the truth," said Connie.

"I don't know," said Lillian. "The little I saw of him made me feel that he was an awfully nice boy. A little moody perhaps, but he did have a lot of charm."

"Two months from now this will all be forgotten," said Connie. "We'll both be laughing at it. I've been through this sort of thing before."

"Sit down a moment, Connie."

Connie sat on the bed.

"I'm going to stick my nose into where it doesn't belong," said Lillian. "Connie, there were so many times in the past when I said exactly what you're saying now—'I'll get over it; I'll keep my pride and I'll get over it; there will be other times and other men! Yes, I suppose time always did make me get over it, but in the end what do I have to show for it? As the years have passed what have I gotten for all my pride?" Pathetically she answered her own question: "Look at me."

The telephone rang.

"I bet that's him," said Lillian.

"Don't be silly!"

"If it is, you be nice to him!" said Lillian.

Connie picked up the receiver. "Hello . . .. Fine, thank you. Well, it got quite late and you were involved with so many people. . . ."

Lillian nodded her head happily and made for the door. Connie waved at her not to leave, but Lillian paid no attention and, with a Cheshire-cat smile, quietly left the room.

"No," said Connie, "I'm going to be busy all day today."

"What about the afternoon?" asked Eddie.

"What did you say? We have a bad connection."

The telephone connection was bad but not that bad. Connie had heard him. She was stalling for time, trying to decide whether to see him again.

"I said what about this afternoon? Will you be free?"

"No. I'm going to be busy all day."

"How about this evening?"

"This evening, too."

"Can you come over to the club later on in the eve ning? We could go out afterwards."

"No, it'll be too late then."

Connie remembered what Lillian had said about giving Eddie a chance to explain his side of the story.

"How about tomorrow?" asked Eddie.

"Well, suppose you call me tomorrow morning, and we'll see."

There was a pause in the conversation. Connie knew that Eddie was wondering about her abrupt attitude.

"If you're angry because of last night," said Eddie, "I'm sorry. But it was impossible for me to break away from all those people. I tried to, and when I finally did you were gone. Wild Man Moore had some business deal he wanted to discuss with me. He said it was important and that's the only reason I went off with him."

"I didn't care about that," said Connie. She could hear Eddie breathing over the phone.

"What is it then?" he asked. To Connie he sounded at that moment like one of her little pupils asking in all innocence why he was being punished, even though he well knew why. She felt like answering him the way she'd answer the pupil—"You know!" But all she said was, "Never mind!"

"What is it?" persisted Eddie. "What are you sore about?"

"Where were you Sunday night?" asked Connie.

"I told you. At a dinner for Wild Man Moore. And after that I went over to your hotel to pick you up."

"And when you didn't find me in? Where did you go then?"

Eddie paused a moment, and then asked, "What difference does that make?"

Suddenly the absurdity of her cross-examining him this way struck her. He wasn't one of her students in school. She had no right to question him as though he had done something wrong. Even if he was lying now and Marie had been telling the truth, he had committed no crime.

"I suppose it really doesn't make any difference," she answered, haltingly.

"Don't you want to see me anymore?" asked Eddie. He sounded almost pathetic. She couldn't help but feel sorry for him.

"Call me tomorrow morning," she said.

"You're sure you can't see me today?"

"Yes."

"We could have dinner together. You could skip the meal at the hotel."

"Call me tomorrow morning."

"All right."

She waited until she heard him hang up, then she put the telephone back on the hook.

She crossed to her bed and flopped face-down on it. She started to cry.

She thought of Lillian's words; Lillian felt the years had left her only regrets and unfulfilled dreams. The old maid schoolteacher—it was proverbial. She remembered several nights before seeing Lillian standing naked in the middle of the room and being somewhat impressed by her figure for her age. And she had an interesting face. All in all, she must have been quite lovely in her younger days. And yet she had never married. Connie wondered if the same fate awaited her.

She stopped crying, sat up, dried her eyes and blew her nose. She was in love with Eddie Cook. That much she knew. How he felt about her was another matter. The way he sounded over the phone a minute ago the troubled catch in his voice—he couldn't have been after her for only one thing, no matter what Marie LeBrun had said.

She washed her face with cold water, put on powder and lipstick and went down to the lobby. Some of the girls had already assembled there. Lillian was talking to two of them. Off to the side stood Mrs. Vogel, Mr. Luften and three other teachers. Since the Saturday night incident in Marie's Cave Mr. Luften had stopped joking with Connie. He looked the other way when he saw her enter the lobby. The others all smiled cheerfully at Connie; they knew about Eddie and felt vicariously excited. When Lillian saw Connie she left the other two teachers and went over to her.

"Well?" she asked.

"I don't know," said Connie. "Let's go over to the other end of the lobby where we can talk."

"Let's not wander too far afield," said Mrs. Vogel in her public voice. "We'll be starting our shopping and buying tour in a little while."

"Somebody ought to buy her a muzzle," said Lillian. "Oh dear," she added, "the way I talk. Paris seems to be bringing out the worst in me. But, tell me, what did he have to say?"

"He wants to see me again."

"Splendid!" exclaimed Lillian, with a happy twinkle in her eye. "You've made a date with him?"

"I told him to call me tomorrow morning."

"Why did you do that?"

"Because I wanted time to think. I'm in love with him, Lillian."

"You're not telling me anything I don't know."

"It's crazy, but I'm going to try to hold on . . . for a while, anyway."

"That's the most sensible thing you've said all day."

"Do you really think I'm doing the right thing?"

"I know you are."

"Then come with me to Mrs. Vogel. There's a very important question I want to ask her."

The two of them marched back across the lobby to Mrs. Vogel.

"Mrs. Vogel, may I speak to you alone for a moment?" asked Connie.

Mrs. Vogel looked surprised, but not nearly as surprised as she looked a moment later, when after stepping off to the side with Connie and Lillian she heard Connie ask, "What's the procedure for staying on in Paris a week or two longer and catching up with the group later?"

"What?" asked Mrs. Vogel, her eyes widening.

"Just what she said," commented Lillian. "We want to know what we have to do if we want to stay on in Paris and catch up with the group later."

⟪20⟫

EDDIE LOOKED at his watch. It was eight A. M., too early to call Connie. He felt foolish. He had shaved, showered, dressed and now had to wait at least an hour before he could call her.

He had returned to his apartment from the club at three, and, after four hours of tossing and turning in bed, pacing the floor, smoking, drinking, standing out on the balcony and watching an occasional truck rumble down the boulevard he had finally given up the idea of trying to get any sleep.

He felt a little more relaxed now but no less troubled. To help kill the hour he decided to pick up the morning newspapers and breakfast outside.

The sky was overcast. The air felt like rain.

"Bonjour, monsieur, you're up early this morning," said the newsstand dealer, looking at Eddie as though Eddie owed him an explanation.

Eddie had nothing to explain. Without bothering to return the newsstand dealer's greeting he plunked down the francs for two French papers and a *Herald Tribune* and walked two blocks to a corner sidewalk restaurant. He sat down and looked for the waiter, who was lowering the huge awning.

"It might rain," said the waiter.

Eddie busied himself with his newspapers. The Algerian situation was worsening; Mendes-France had made a speech attacking the government's handling of the Middle East situation; there was a severe sugar shortage because of hoarding; and Poujade was still sending out anti-Semitic literature.

"Monsieur?"

Eddie looked up from his newspaper. "Coffee and bread and butter."

The waiter left. Eddie saw two small boys pass by, each carrying a three-foot loaf of French bread. Behind them came a young woman wheeling a baby carriage. She was very good-looking. Her few-months-old baby smiled at Eddie. The mother noticed it and she too smiled. Eddie recalled that several times recently, wandering through the parks and observing young mothers with their children, he had felt that as a group young mothers were probably the most attractive women of all. He wondered whether feeling this way meant that a settling-down quality was finally coming out in him. He recalled that as a kid any mother seemed like an old lady to him. As he grew older, people he once considered ancient now seemed comparatively young. It was all relative, he supposed, all part of the process of growing up.

The young mother and her infant passed out of sight. Eddie wondered what her husband was like. He knew he wasn't a jazz musician. It was odd how three of the boys in the band had married in Paris and none of them had any children.

He lit a cigarette and left the pack lying on the table. He had a mental image of himself and Connie walking down the boulevard with a baby carriage.

He thought about the telephone call to Connie the morning before. It had upset him terribly. She had sounded sharp with him, as though she didn't want to see him again. It was strange how she had questioned him about where he had gone Sunday night. She couldn't have found out that he had been with Marie. But even if she had found out, although he was sure she hadn't, what difference should that make to her? After all she was leaving Paris on Friday. She must know that meant the end of their brief relationship. Certainly, he had acted coolly enough toward her on Monday, when all they did was visit the Cirque d'Hiver. What difference should it make to her?

And what difference should it make to him? Why did he let the fact that she had sounded peeved on the phone, that she had refused to see him yesterday, upset him for the entire day and night?

It was ironic how Connie's change in attitude, her coldness and indifference had hurt his vanity and self-confidence, had made him want to see her more than ever.

The waiter arrived with Eddie's breakfast. Eddie looked at his watch. Time was crawling.

The two of them sat inside the Pam-Pam Bar at the table where they first met. It was Connie's idea. Eddie was having his second cup of coffee with her, his fifth cup of coffee that morning. He was more upset and confused than ever. He had expected to find her as abrupt and unfriendly as she had been the day before on the phone. He knew that this would have displeased him, made him uncomfortable, but her new attitude, eager and cheerful, proved even more disturbing. Outside it had begun to rain lightly.

She slipped her hand into his. "You know," she said, "you've not only made my visit to Paris more interesting, but the visits of all the girls in the group. You've given them something to gossip about, and how they love it."

"It's too bad they have to rely on gossip for their amusement," said Eddie.

Eddie looked at Connie carefully. He remembered thinking when he first met her that while she was extremely attractive she wasn't really beautiful. He felt different now. There was a quiet soft beauty about her, more meaningful and lasting than the superficial flashiness which was sometimes mistaken for beauty. Her eyes were soft and kind, and her hand was soft and wonderful to hold. Still, sitting with her here, he felt uneasy and depressed.

"Yes," she continued, "thanks to you, I've become quite a scandal. And when I told Mrs. Vogel yesterday that I wanted to stay on in Paris another week or so and catch up with the group later, that was the last straw. I'm sure they think that I'm a completely lost woman and they'll never see me again."

Inadvertently, he drew his hand away from hers. "Stay on? You mean you're not leaving on Friday?"

"That's right," she said. "Both Lillian and I have decided to stay on. You don't seem very pleased about it."

"Why shouldn't I be pleased?" he asked.

"I don't know," Connie replied, "but you seem sort of upset . . . and frightened."

"Frightened? Don't be ridiculous."

Connie no longer looked cheerful. She looked disappointed and hurt. "My staying on doesn't mean we have to continue seeing each other," she said.

Eddie felt hemmed in, as though he had to escape. He didn't know what he wanted. He did know that it would be unfair to play with her emotions this way any longer.

"Of course I'd like to see you while you're in Paris," he began, "but—but I don't want to mislead you. I—I just hope you haven't decided to stay on in Paris on my account. I mean, well, as you yourself have said we're all sort of a lost tribe over here."

Connie was silent a moment. She hardly moved but when she spoke to him her voice was strained. "Perhaps you're assuming a lot. Perhaps you're assuming too much."

Her voice cracked and she started to cry as she said, "What makes you think you're the reason I've decided to stay on in Paris!" She turned away and covered her eyes with her hand and tried to hold back the tears. Eddie moved to her side and put his arm around her. She tried moving away from him.

"Let me alone!" she said. "What do you want from me? What do you want from me?"

Eddie couldn't stand to see her cry. He held her close. "I want you to say that you decided to stay on in Paris because of me," he said. "I want you to say it because I love you. Yes, I love you and that's why you're right, I *am* afraid, because I've never fallen in love with anyone like you before and I don't know what to do about it. But I do know that I love you and I want you to stop crying and I want to put my arms around you and kiss you."

He pressed his cheek against hers and she sniffed back the tears and said, "Not here, not here."

Another couple had entered the restaurant and sat down near them and stared at them. They were obviously American tourists. The waiter shook his head sadly and said to Eddie in French, "It's raining outside, where could I put them?"

Eddie signaled for the bill, paid it, told the waiter to keep the change and said to Connie, who had quieted down, "Let's get out of here."

Connie opened her purse, took out her handkerchief and dried her eyes. "Where can we go?" she asked. "It's raining."

"We'll go over to my place."

The waiter moved the table away to let them slip out of their seats.

Connie waited inside the entrance while Eddie, his jacket collar turned up, went out into the street to get a cab. They hardly talked as the cab made its way through the rain and the traffic to Eddie's apartment house.

Once inside, Eddie poured Connie a drink and, without saying anything, she took it. Then she said, "It's the first time I've ever had a drink this early in the morning."

"It's only to keep from catching cold," said Eddie. He poured himself one. "To us," he toasted, and gulped it down.

"I'm sorry I cried before," said Connie.

"That's all right." He crossed to the windows and opened the blinds. "It certainly turned out to be a nasty day."

"You can leave the blinds closed if you want to," said Connie.

"Are you sure?"

"Yes."

He lowered the blinds again.

«21»

STANDING AT the top of the ladder on the back of the bus the driver was placing on the rack the luggage handed to him by one of the hotel porters. Mrs. Vogel and her teachers, holding on to their small handpieces and their coats, stood outside the hotel watching. Mr. Luften was saying good-by to Mrs. Vogel. Connie, Lillian and Martin Weiner stood off to the side.

"Don't put my valise on the bottom!" screamed one of the teachers who had been carefully scrutinizing the luggage operation. "You always put my valise on the bottom and it gets crushed. Put it on top of someone else's valise this time!"

Obligingly the driver shifted the luggage around. "Don't put it on top of mine!" shouted another teacher. No matter how the luggage was loaded there were still some complaints.

"Yeah," said Martin Weiner, "I saw the girls again last night. Very nice girls." He turned to Lillian. "I sure wanted to see your musician friend again to thank him for introducing me to those girls. They were the only people I met here who didn't make me feel like a tourist. A visitor, yes, but not like a tourist. Being able to get into people's homes makes all the difference."

Yes, Connie thought, it does make the difference. Certainly *she* hadn't felt like a tourist, thanks to Eddie.

She wondered how Eddie had reacted to the letter she had sent him. Perhaps she should have told him face to face why she had decided to leave Paris on schedule after all. But she knew that face to face she wouldn't have had the courage or the strength to tell him what she had written in the letter.

"Yeah," said Martin Weiner, "those girls your musician friend introduced me to were a lot more interesting than some of the creeps in this group. Present company, of course, excluded."

Connie looked at the girls in the group. She felt sorry for herself, she felt sorry for Eddie, but most of all she felt sorry for them. Several of the girls were married but the fact that they had decided to leave their husbands for the ten weeks of the trip didn't speak well of their marriages; two or three of the girls were divorced; there was one widow; and the rest of the group were single-old maid schoolteachers; she was sure that not one of them had had an experience comparable to her own during this Paris sojourn.

"Next time I come to Europe, without the benefit of any tour, thank you, I'll spend more time in Paris," said Martin Weiner. "I don't know why you two changed your minds about staying on. First you decide to stay and then you decide to go. I don't get it. If I had the money I'd stay on, that's for sure. What made you two change your minds again?"

Lillian, looking sympathetically at Connie, said, "Don't ask so many questions."

They watched the driver place the last piece of luggage on the rack. He began covering the luggage with tarpaulin.

"You coming inside?" asked Martin Weiner.

"In a minute," said Lillian.

"Well, I'm going inside now so I can get a seat near the window," said Martin. "I wonder if we'll really get those box lunches Mrs. Vogel promised us."

"Don't be such a skeptic," said Lillian.

Martin climbed in the bus.

"If you want to change your mind again," said Lillian, "you better do it now before he ties everything down."

"Can you imagine the fit Mrs. Vogel would really have if we told her we'd changed our minds again?" said Connie.

"Don't worry about Mrs. Vogel," said Lillian, "worry about yourself—and Eddie."

"I have been," said Connie. "That's why we're leaving Paris now." She opened her handbag and took out the unopened pack of English cigarettes she had bought earlier that morning—the same brand Eddie smoked. She lit one.

"I suppose you know what you're doing," said Lillian, "although, as I said before, I don't quite understand it."

Peter had the tarpaulin in place, threw some ropes across it and began tying it all down. Most of the teachers had taken their seats in the bus.

"Well I guess we might as well go inside, too," said Lillian.

"You go on ahead," said Connie. "Save me a seat. I want to finish my cigarette."

"Do you want to sit near the window?"

"It makes no difference to me."

Two porters came out of the hotel carrying the box lunches. Lillian followed them into the bus.

Connie looked down the street, wondering what her reaction would be if Eddie were suddenly to appear, knowing that he wouldn't, hoping that he would.

She wondered whether she would ever see him again. She had included her Chicago address in the letter.

Thinking back on what she had written she realized how difficult it had been to express herself. She wondered whether Eddie would truly understand. She had spoken of their love, but had raised the question of how long it would last with the one big problem between them unresolved. She could never be happy living in Paris with him as an expatriate, and his returning to the States would never work out if it was done solely because of her. If he returned, it had to be because he realized he belonged there, despite all the things he hated about it, despite all the bad breaks he'd had there; that's where his roots were, that's where his people were, that's where he belonged. And that was why she had to leave him now. He had to have time to work these things out for himself.

Mrs. Vogel and Mr. Luften approached Connie. "And good-by to you, too," said Mr. Luften. "You keep an eye on her, Mrs. Vogel. She's the wild one in this group. In every group there's always at least one. That's been my observation."

Mr. Luften extended his hand. Connie didn't feel like taking it but to avoid a scene she shook hands with him. She didn't like the way his eyes gave her the once-over as he squeezed her hand with what she considered unnecessary pressure. To get away from him and to avoid having to say anything further to Mrs. Vogel she entered the bus and sat down next to Lillian.

One of the teachers who had been with Connie and Lillian in Marie's Cave sat behind them. She hunched over and, pointing through the window to Mrs. Vogel and Mr. Luften still gabbing outside, said, "I don't think Connie's the only one who's had a little romantic interlude in Paris. If you ask me I think something's been going on between those two."

Lillian laughed. "They suit one another anyway. That's one thing for sure."

A romantic interlude, thought Connie. Was that all it would add up to? She hoped not. She wondered what Eddie's reaction to the letter had been, if he understood her, if he believed her, or if he felt that there was some other reason for her deciding to run away. She had examined her motivations as honestly as she knew how; she herself was convinced that there was no reason other than the one she had given him: time to make up his own mind. She knew she'd be far happier if she had remained on in Paris than she was going to be during the next few weeks. But this was the way things had to be. Mr. Luften and Mrs. Vogel entered the bus.

"Just a final good-by," said Mr. Luften. "I hope you have a wonderful trip and all the men you meet on the Riviera look just like Gregory Peck!"

A few of the girls laughed. They always did, thought Connie, no matter what the fool said.

"See you all again next year," said Mr. Luften and, giving Mrs. Vogel his final handshake, he jumped out of the bus.

"When do we eat?" called out one of the teachers, jokingly. Again there was laughter. They had finished breakfast a little while ago.

"Right after Fontainebleau," said Mrs. Vogel. "We should be there in about two hours. The tour of the Palace will take a little over an hour and then we'll have our box lunches in the park just outside the Palace. It will be very pleasant. The city of Dijon will be our first overnight stop. Dijon, as you know, is famous for mustard but, more than that, for its Burgundy cooking."

Connie hoped that the driver would start the bus and put an end to Mrs. Vogel's prattle.

"Dijon is the heart of the Burgundy region and this evening we're going to see a Comédie-Française production of *Tartuffe* in the courtyard of the Palace of the Duke of Burgundy. I'm sure you all remember the Duke of Burgundy from that song . . ." and here she started to sing off-key . . . "Sons of toil and danger, will you serve a stranger, and bow down to Burgundy!"

"Oh, God!" said Lillian.

"Anyway," continued Mrs. Vogel, "it's in the Palace of the Duke of Burgundy that we're going to see *Tartuffe*."

"Is this one of the *extras?*" asked one of the teachers.

Extras were activities not listed on the itinerary, which Teachers Tours, Inc. provided free of charge. Nobody knew what they were or when they would occur, except that there were supposed to be three or four of them during the tour. Of course Mrs. Vogel knew but she thought it would be more amusing to surprise the group with them from time to time. So far, there had been no *extras.*

"If you'd read your itinerary more carefully," said Mrs. Vogel, "you'd see that the play is listed on it. And your ticket for admission happens to be Blue Coupon number thirty-four."

Although her cigarette was only half finished Connie no longer felt like smoking. She crushed it out in the ash tray that was on the back of the seat in front of her. By now all of the teachers were in the bus. Most of them were nervously chattering away with one another. Some were reading magazines or looking up Dijon in their guidebooks.

Connie sat in silence, peering out of the window at the hotel she would soon see no more, the hotel at which Eddie had called for her, the hotel to which he had delivered her, the hotel where one night, Lillian, more drunk than she had probably been in her entire life, gushed forth her wild adventures of the evening with a pianist named Benny. She was thankful that Lillian knew enough not to talk to her now.

She wondered what Eddie was doing at this moment, whether he was up yet, whether he was thinking of her as she was thinking of him. She wondered what he would be doing later on in the day, later on in the week, and in the weeks and months to come. Then the terrifying thought came to her again that perhaps he hadn't received her letter. This thought had come to her yesterday and she had dismissed it. No, there was no such possibility. He had received the letter. If he hadn't received it he certainly would have telephoned her. When, late Wednesday afternoon, he took her from his apartment back to her hotel it was understood that he would be getting in touch with her the next day. And that night she wrote the letter. And the next morning, Thursday morning, he undoubtedly received it. And that was why there had been no word from him. The next move had to be his.

Climbing into his seat the driver shut the door and started the motor and the excitement of departure ran through the bus. Mr. Luften stood on the sidewalk outside the hotel, smiling broadly and waving good-by. Two of the hotel porters stood alongside him, neither smiling nor waving, their somber faces revealing their general apathy and their particular displeasure at the size of the tips they had received. A few curious passers-by stopped for a moment and also stood on the street watching. As the bus pulled slowly away from the curb the teachers jumped up from their seats and peered out of the windows to get a final look at the hotel, at Mr. Luften, at the porters and passers-by. Not until the bus progressed down the avenue did they sit back in their seats. For a moment they were calm; each time a familiar landmark came into view, a museum or monument they had visited, the Seine, the Eiffel Tower, they gleefully pointed it out and shrilly chatted away. At the outskirts of the city the bus picked up speed as it hit the main highway, and before long they were out of the city completely, seeing fields and woods, on their way to Fontainebleau.

Connie took her eyes away from the window and saw that Lillian was staring at her.

"Connie," said Lillian, "I'm going to ask you a very personal question. I've never asked anyone this question before and you don't have to answer it if you don't want to."

"What is it?" asked Connie.

It was obvious that Lillian was terribly nervous and apprehensive about asking it.

"Did you and Eddie . . . well, did you and Eddie have an affair?"

"You mean did we sleep together?"

Lillian blushed. Slowly she nodded.

"Yes," replied Connie.

"I'm glad," said Lillian. "I'm terribly glad. I'm going to tell you something that I've never told anyone before." She had to swallow before she could say it. "I've never had an affair with a man—never in my whole life. I guess that makes me out to be something of a freak."

At that moment Connie thought her heart would break for Lillian. She had never seen Lillian looking so pathetic or sad. Two tears rolled down her face. Connie placed her hand on Lillian's and squeezed gently. "Don't be silly," Connie said, "don't be silly."

Lillian, looking ashamed, sank down in her chair and turned her head toward the window. Connie kept her hand on Lillian's and looked across the aisle through the other window. She now knew for sure that no matter what lay ahead, meeting Eddie Cook had been the most wonderful thing that had ever happened to her.

《22》

FOR WHAT must have been the hundredth time Eddie read Connie's letter. He understood it no better than the first time he had read it.

No doubt by now Connie and her group had left Paris and were on their way to the south of France. He called the hotel.

"Hello."

"Miss Connie Mitchell, please."

"She has checked out."

"Have they all left?"

"All the schoolteachers, you mean? The group from Teachers Tours?"

"Yes."

"Yes, they left in their bus early this morning. They are going to the Riviera."

"Thank you very much."

He hung up. He felt a wave of relief that was similar to the one he had felt when he first read her letter. The letter had lifted a great weight from his shoulders. It had meant that he was not obliged to see her or even call her any more. And the phone call he had just made, confirming that she had left, meant that it was final.

He wondered how deeply he could be in love with her if he felt only relief at her leaving him.

His first interpretation of the letter had been that she had suddenly changed her mind because she was frightened; despite her protestations about capricious affairs and one-night stands her bourgeois background wouldn't permit an extended relationship unless there was a guarantee of future marriage. He had felt this about

211

her and, while they were making love, to allay her fears, to put her more at ease, out of both sympathy and love for her, he had told her that there was a good possibility of his coming back to the States with her. And he had meant it at the time. But she must have known that he had meant it only *at the time.*

And this was his second and more lasting reaction to her letter— that she had written to release him from any obligations she felt she might have imposed upon him, to let him off the hook. She meant what she had written and he was thankful to her for it.

It felt good to be free again, to be able to go back to the way things were and always would be, to be able to go back to Marie. The affair with Connie was at an end. He would never completely forget her— he knew that. He would think about her from time to time, and sometimes thinking about her would bring on a loneliness and a deep wanting and regret—that had happened before—but then, gradually, he would think about her less and less until finally, she would have become only a souvenir of the past.

Meanwhile he had her letter and he kept reading it over and over again. There was no point, he knew, in doing this. It would be better to throw the letter away. But he didn't. Instead he put it for the time being at the bottom of one of his dresser drawers.

He crossed to the window and looked out. The overcast sky was beginning to clear slightly. He felt a brisk walk would be good for him. He put on his jacket and started out for Marie's Cave.

When he arrived there he was about to go right up to Marie's apartment but hesitated a moment, because he heard voices in the club itself. He pushed through the swinging door and saw three men, one in a beret, one in a fedora and the other hatless, seated at one of the tables pouring over blueprints. Eddie didn't know who they were but one of them recognized him immediately.

"Ah, Monsieur Eddie Cook!" exclaimed the man with the beret. "Perhaps you can help us."

"What's going on?"

"He's the man who plays such marvelous music here," said the man with the beret to the others. They shook hands with Eddie.

"We have a problem," said the man with the fedora. "We're trying to figure out how to break through that wall and expand the club to more than twice its size without disturbing business."

"I've hit upon a good idea," said the man who had recognized Eddie. "We'll start in the other room and leave the wall intact. In other words we'll work completely from the other side. Then, when everything's finished except the wall we'll tear that down one night in a special celebration before all the guests. Won't that be a marvelous stunt? Think of the publicity."

"I keep telling him it's impractical," said the man with the fedora, "because with the expanded space the bandstand will have to be relocated. But he won't listen to reason."

"We can worry about that later," said the man with the beret.

Eddie left the two of them arguing and ran up the steps to Marie's apartment. The door was open and Marie was in and alone. She had on an ermine-topped black lounging robe. They kissed and she closed and locked the door.

"So you're going through with the plans for expanding the club after all," said Eddie.

"I told you I was," she said.

"I had no idea it was to be this soon."

"We want to have it finished before the end of the present tourist season."

"I still don't like the idea," protested Eddie. "Why can't things be left as they are?"

"Oh, Eddie, my pet, let's not talk about that now. I'm so glad you came. I just called you, as a matter of fact. I didn't know you were on your way over here. I missed you so these past few days. Have you been avoiding me?"

"Of course not."

"Then kiss me."

He took her in his arms and kissed her. She kept her arms around him but pulled her face away from his. "Nobody's forcing you to, you know. If you don't want to . . ."

He kissed her again. Playfully, she pushed herself away from him. She was obviously in high spirits. She raised her arms above her head and started doing a slow grind. She started to sing:

> I've got a man, he treats me terribly mean,
> I've got a man, he treats me terribly mean,
> If he still loves me remains to be seen!

"Voice isn't too bad, is it?" Marie asked.

Eddie thought that the undulating body was a lot better than the undulating voice but he said, "Not bad at all."

"Of course I would never go back to singing professionally," she said. "I'm way beyond that. But I thought I might do a few numbers at a party once in a while."

"Might not be a bad idea," said Eddie. He thought it was an awful idea. He couldn't keep his eyes off her body, which she was now subtly swaying back and forth. Yes, thought Eddie, it was ridiculous of him ever to have thought of getting involved with Connie. It was even more ridiculous for him and Marie ever to have broken up, to have stopped seeing one another. Why had they? He didn't want to think about that now.

"You know," said Marie, "I feel the way I did when we first started. It's funny, isn't it?"

She took off her robe. She had nothing on underneath. "How do you feel about it?"

"Let's go inside, " said Eddie.

The bedroom door suddenly opened. It was Marie's English maid. She had intended to come into the room but, seeing her mistress in the state she was in, hesitated.

"It's all right," said Marie, as cool and controlled as ever. She handed the maid her robe. "Hang this up," she said. The maid took the robe and hung it in the closet. Eddie noticed that she didn't seem unduly embarrassed and he couldn't help but wonder how many times before she had seen Marie in a compromising position and with how many other men. For the moment he didn't care.

Marie looked at him meaningfully. "Well?" she asked. She walked into the bedroom. He followed her in.

They had both showered and he had dressed and they sat in the living room being served tea by the maid. Eddie said, "I'll tell you another reason I don't like the idea of your expanding the club. It'll put you deeper in debt to Varay. He'll be hanging around all the time. He'll be a bigger nuisance than ever."

Marie smiled as she buttered a slice of toast. Eddie expected her to say something but she didn't. She merely continued to smile. He didn't like it.

"You wouldn't want him hanging around that much now, would you? Not now."

"I wanted to wait a while before telling you this," said Marie, looking away from Eddie while she talked, "but I suppose I better tell it to you now. Actually it needn't affect us, I mean our relationship, one bit."

Then she looked at Eddie and said matter-of-factly, "Varay and I are going to get married."

Unbelievable though it sounded Eddie knew immediately that Marie was telling the truth. It fitted into her pattern of change, her sudden interest in new things—new door chimes, new tape recorder, new hair-do, new nightclub, and now new husband.

"As I said, it needn't affect us."

Eddie felt the fool. All his renewed pleasure in Marie suddenly and completely vanished. Their relationship meant absolutely nothing now, nothing more than animal satisfaction. All the things he hated about Marie—her vanity, prejudices, snobbishness—things he had pushed out of his consciousness during their reunion, now came vividly to mind. He remembered a dozen telling incidents. They had been so convenient to forget. His view of her was painfully yanked into its proper perspective. He felt enraged—not so much at her as at himself.

"Well," said Marie, "aren't you going to congratulate me? It's not every day I marry a Count."

"Why are you doing it?" asked Eddie.

"Eddie, how naive can you be? Do you know how much money he has? Do you know what his connections are? Do you know that marrying him would establish me in society?"

"And, of course, he's white."

"What has that to do with it?" snapped Marie.

"Nothing. But with you he'd have to be white."

Her face became tense for a moment, then relaxed as she took control of herself. "Let's not quarrel," she said. "I don't love Varay and you know it. The marriage is one of convenience. What Varay won't know won't hurt him. And even if he did know it might not make any difference to him. He's very broadminded. As long as he can have me once in a while that's all he wants. Meanwhile you and I can be together again."

She sipped her tea and called to the maid, "Bring us more toast. Would you like anything else?" she asked Eddie.

He didn't answer.

"Stop looking at me like that."

"Well, Marie, I've got to hand it to you. You knew what you wanted and went out and got it. First it was the intellectuals—the writers, the artists. Now it's high society, big money, a Count. You finally made it, Marie. You proved you could marry a white man. And a Count, too."

Marie grabbed her cup of tea and threw it at him. He moved aside and it went crashing into the wall behind him.

Eddie stood up and, as he did so, knocked over both the table and Marie. The maid heard the crash and came running in and gasped hysterically. Marie lay sprawled out on the floor, her robe torn open. It was obvious that she was more stunned than hurt. She didn't even attempt to cover herself but lay there panting fearfully, extending an arm toward her maid to be helped up.

Eddie laughed. "You certainly don't look like a Countess now," he said. He no longer felt enraged. Marie looked positively ludicrous. He stepped toward her to help her.

"Don't touch me!" she growled. As the maid started to help her to her feet she backed away from Eddie and fell down again. Once more Eddie laughed.

"Call the police," Marie screamed. "Call the police!"

Eddie walked out of the apartment.

«23»

THE NEXT day Eddie called the Aisle de Charenton hospital and was told by Dr. Kaval that Michel was still there. He decided to visit him.

Michel was as concerned as ever about his letters of recommendation, about why he hadn't heard from Stravinsky. There was no improvement.

Dr. Kaval, as before, was congenial. As Eddie sat in his small office the psychiatrist told him that they would try shock treatments on Michel if they could get Michel's brother to consent to them.

"Why won't he?" asked Eddie.

"I don't know," said Dr. Kaval. "We are having a difficult time trying to contact him. He seems uninterested in his brother's welfare."

"I'll get to him," said Eddie. "And if I can't get to him I'll get to someone else in the family."

"It's very kind of you to take such an interest in him. Is he a good friend of yours?"

"Well," said Eddie, "not really. It was hard to get to know him. He was always a little—well, peculiar."

The psychiatrist smiled. "Do you live in Paris?"

"Yes."

"You speak French very well. Have you been here a long time?"

"Twelve years."

"I suppose you find it much more tolerable than living in America."

"It has its advantages."

"Discrimination must be a terrible thing there," said Dr. Kaval.

"It is."

"But things seem to be changing for the better. The bus boycotts in the South. The Negroes sending their children to the newly integrated schools despite the violence. I think it's wonderful that the American Negroes are finally demanding their rights. They should have done it earlier."

"It's pretty difficult to demand your rights when you know that if you do your house may be blown up."

"They're doing it just the same, though, aren't they?"

Eddie lit a cigarette. He offered one to Dr. Kaval.

"No, thank you. I've recently stopped smoking."

"The cancer scare?"

"Partly. But also because it saves expense. We psychiatrists don't make much in France."

"You ought to go to America," said Eddie, putting his pack of cigarettes away. "Everyone goes to psychiatrists in America. To get back to Michel, you still don't know what made him crack up?"

"Not really."

"As I said, he always was a little peculiar."

"So are a lot of other people who never become insane. His illness may have a purely physical basis."

"Do you think the shock treatments will help?"

"There's a good chance that they will."

"I'll go over to see his family right away."

"Good," said Dr. Kaval. "I'll give you their address."

Sitting in the Metro on the way over to Michel's brother's house Eddie felt resentful toward Dr. Kaval for speaking to him about discrimination back in the States. Many Frenchmen spoke to him about the problems of Negroes back in America. They never assumed that having lived in France for twelve years he was no longer interested in what was happening back in America, that the problems of racial discrimination were the problems of American Negroes, not his problems and, now, sitting in the subway among all the French people, he realized how much separated him from them, even though he had lived among them for twelve years. He knew that Dr. Kaval was right—the problems of the American Negroes were still his problems. No matter how long he remained in France, even if it was for the rest of his life, he would always be an American whether he liked it or not. The French would always consider him an American and, more important, he would always consider himself an American. ("You may be able to talk our language perfectly," the French police official had said, "but you'll never be able to speak it.")

This was what Connie knew and this was why she had made such an issue of his returning to the States. And this was probably why, he reasoned, he had felt relieved when he received her letter—not having to face Connie meant that he didn't have to face his problem. How wrong he was! And, now, how he missed Connie. How he missed her!

When he arrived at the address given him by Dr. Kaval and spoke to Michel's brother, the words were about Michel, about how important it was for the brother to give his consent to the shock treatments, but the thoughts were of Connie.

He could think about Connie and, at the same time, speak in no uncertain terms to Michel's brother. Thinking about Connie seemed to give him the strength to be forthright and convincing about Michel.

"All right," agreed the brother, "I'll give my permission for the shock treatments. I still don't understand why you're that concerned about Michel. He's my brother, not yours. As a matter of fact, I should resent—"

"I don't care what you should or shouldn't resent," interrupted Eddie. "I don't particularly care how you think or feel about anything. I'm only interested in your seeing that your brother receives the proper medical attention."

"I just told you that I would attend to it," said the brother, annoyed.

"You better," said Eddie, and he left the apartment.

Standing in the hall waiting for the elevator he thought of the words of Michel's brother: "I still don't understand why you're so concerned about Michel." Why was he so concerned? He wondered whether it was only because of Michel or because he saw in this strange, lonely, self-tortured French Negro something of himself.

The self-service elevator arrived and Eddie stepped inside.

He walked for about an hour, until he came to a café that was a hangout for musicians. Benny was there and in a very excited state. When he saw Eddie he broke away from the other musicians to whom he had been talking and, gesticulating wildly, ran over to Eddie.

"Why didn't you tell me?" demanded Benny.

"Tell you what?"

"We've been canned! We've all been canned! You knew!"

"I didn't."

"I dropped by there this morning to pick up some music one of the boys wanted to borrow and Marie blew a gasket screaming at me to get the hell out and never come back. Some guys were ripping the joint apart and one of them said something about making the place bigger and Marie yelled that the club would be closed for two weeks but that didn't make any difference as far as we were concerned. She said that we were through for good. She said that if I saw you I should tell you to have the boys pick up their instruments. How do you like that! I wonder what brought it on all of a sudden!"

"You're not worried, are you?" asked Eddie.

"Are you kiddin'? We'll have fifty offers by tonight, and better deals than we got from Marie."

"Let's sit down," said Eddie. "I'll buy you a drink."

They took a table away from the bar and Eddie waited until Benny was halfway through his drink before he asked, "What would you think about going back to the States?"

Obviously Benny was shocked by the question. "The whole band?"

"If they want to come," said Eddie.

"I doubt that; I doubt that very much."

"How about you?" asked Eddie.

"Did you and Marie have a fight? It must've been a beaut!"

"What do you think?" asked Eddie. "Would you want to go back?"

"Or is it because of that schoolteacher chick?"

"Answer my question," said Eddie.

"Buy me another drink," said Benny. He gulped down the one he had and Eddie ordered him another one.

"I think you're making a big mistake," said Benny, "if you're thinking of going back. Have you forgotten what it's like?"

"No."

"And it would be tougher for you than it would be for me. You wouldn't be able to live where you wanted to, you—"

"I know all that," interrupted Eddie. "I know how it would be, how much tougher even because I've been away from it all for twelve years."

"Then why? *Why?*"

"I'm not sure."

"Must be that schoolteacher chick!"

"Maybe."

"Would you see her if you went back?"

"Yes."

The waiter brought over Benny's drink.

"But how about you?" asked Eddie. "How about your going back with me?"

Benny stared for a moment at his drink, then said thoughtfully, "All my friends are here. I've made a life for myself here. I've nothing to go back for."

"We could work together there."

"No, Eddie, I just couldn't go back." He looked at Eddie with sad eyes.

"Then I guess I'll be going back alone."

"When do you think that'll be?"

"Pretty soon, I guess."

Benny lifted his drink in a toast, his hand trembling. "Here's to you," he said.